"I Want the Contract, but I Don't Want to Have to See You on a Daily Basis to Get It."

Courtney held her breath, waiting for the explosion.

Shoving the car into park, Kace turned to face her. His eyes were dark and unreadable. "I realize I ought to be upset with you for your childish stunt. . . . But," he continued, ignoring Courtney's gasp, "I know you haven't as yet come to terms with what's between us, so I'm going to overlook it and pretend it never happened."

A cold shudder went through Courtney. "Now you listen to me, Kace McCord! I—"

"Didn't anyone ever tell you that you also talk too much?" he interrupted savagely. Before Courtney knew what was happening, she was in his arms, responding wildly to his passionate kiss. *1-6-1982*

MARY LYNN BAXTER

owns and operates the D&B Book Store in Lufkin, Texas. Romances have been her favorite books for years, and she sells more romances than any other type of book.

Dear Reader:

SILHOUETTE DESIRE is an exciting new line of contemporary romances from Silhouette Books. During the past year, many Silhouette readers have written in telling us what other types of stories they'd like to read from Silhouette, and we've kept these comments and suggestions in mind in developing SILHOUETTE DESIRE.

DESIREs feature all of the elements you like to see in a romance, plus a more sensual, provocative story. So if you want to experience all the excitement, passion and joy of falling in love, then SILHOUETTE DESIRE is for you.

I hope you enjoy this book and all the wonderful stories to come from SILHOUETTE DESIRE. I'd appreciate any thoughts you'd like to share with us on new SILHOUETTE DESIRE, and I invite you to write to us at the address below:

Karen Solem
Editor-in-Chief
Silhouette Books
P.O. Box 769
New York, N.Y. 10019

MARY LYNN BAXTER
Shared Moments

Silhouette Desire
Published by Silhouette Books New York
America's Publisher of Contemporary Romance

Other Silhouette Books by Mary Lynn Baxter

All Our Tomorrows
Tears of Yesterday

SILHOUETTE BOOKS, a Simon & Schuster Division of
GULF & WESTERN CORPORATION
1230 Avenue of the Americas, New York, N.Y. 10020

Copyright © 1982 by Mary Lynn Baxter

Distributed by Pocket Books

ISBN: 0-671-44368-2

First Silhouette Books printing October, 1982

10 9 8 7 6 5 4 3 2 1

America's Publisher of Contemporary Romance

Printed in the U.S.A.

1

~~~~~~~~~~~~~~~

Courtney took one look at Kace McCord and knew that he spelled trouble.

It wasn't because he was one of the handsomest men she had ever seen in her life. She had seen other men with dark blue eyes and silver-gray hair who were just as pleasing to the eye. No, it was the way he looked at her.

As he uncurled his gangly frame from behind his desk, his interested gaze began at the tip of her toes and worked slowly upward. It missed nothing of her one hundred fifteen–pound frame, scrutinizing her long legs, lingering upon her breasts, taking in the mass of blue-black hair she had spent half an hour arranging.

He grinned warmly, too warmly, she thought, as she gripped the handle of her briefcase hard. She felt her nails cutting into her palms. This man's bold stare unnerved her. Her insides hadn't quivered like this since that fateful night so long ago.

7

For a moment she didn't know whether to remain in the doorway of his office and try to get the contract or leave and run out into the streets of New Orleans like a coward. Courtney Roberts, get a hold of yourself! You're a grown woman of twenty-nine! Your business needs what this man has to offer, even if all six-feet-plus of him *is* the devil in khakis.

"You can come in, Miss Roberts. I promise I won't bite."

"Are you sure of that, Mr. McCord?" she questioned with a slight tremor in her voice. She swung her briefcase around and clutched it to her stomach.

"Yes, I'm sure," he teased as his hands let the blueprints roll shut with a rustling clatter. "I only bite young women with brown eyes. I can't tell whether yours are more gray or more green." His eyes narrowed as they locked with Courtney's, searching, probing.

For a moment Courtney was taken aback at his personal remarks and his hungry look. She resented his attitude of familiarity, and she berated herself for letting him get to her. Since Hal's betrayal, she had kept men at bay—all men. They made nice escorts for dinner and parties and were a good excuse to buy designer clothes and handy at repairing cars and carrying heavy boxes. She enjoyed laughing at their jokes and liked their companionship, but that was as far as she allowed any relationship to go. She was satisfied with her life the way it was. Her lovely condominium and her sportscar had been paid for with her own money. She didn't want to change anything about her lifestyle. And she had *no* intention of returning two hundred wedding presents ever again!

Through clenched teeth she said, "Mr. McCord, it does

not matter what color my eyes are. I'm here to talk business."

Unruffled, he grinned. He didn't take his eyes off her as he made his way around the desk and leaned up against its edge. "All right, you win. We'll talk business if you'll have a seat." His grin widened as he began unconsciously to swing his leg from side to side in a hypnotizing manner.

Courtney felt her face grow red at the blatant invitation written on his face. She had never met anyone who exuded such an aura of raw masculinity. She was confused and totally lost as to how to handle such a strong "come-on" from this man whose contract could mean the future success of her business.

As Courtney lowered herself onto the plush office chair adjacent to his desk, Amy's words of caution bounced through her mind: "Courtney, remember to tread lightly. You're destined to meet your match in Kace McCord." She had scoffed at those words from her trusted assistant and friend, Amy Neal. Courtney felt she could handle any man. Now, as she sat before him, she was less confident. Doubt circled her already befuddled senses like a clouded mist. She shook her head several times before she could bring herself to look at him.

Thoughtfully sensing her agitation, Kace became serious—all business. He leaned across his desk and reached for the folder marked "Paper-Work-Plus" and began thumbing through it.

Not raising his head, he remarked politely, "I'm sorry, Miss Roberts, I haven't had a chance to check your company or your qualifications. If you'll bear with me a moment, I'll take a quick look."

Courtney swallowed her irritation. "By all means, take

your time." She was pressed to keep the sarcasm out of her voice. Amy had gone to the trouble to send him a copy of their requirements a week ago, and he hadn't even bothered to check them. She had felt certain the job would be hers. Now a knot of uncertainty was forming in her stomach.

While he studied her file, she had a free perusal of this rugged and good-looking owner of McCord Builders, Inc. She judged him to be in his early to mid-forties, although the silvery hair that crowned his well-shaped head made him seem older than he probably was. His khaki shirt and pants molded the wide expanse of his shoulders and the lean but muscled trimness of his hips to perfection. His dark tan, heightened by the dazzling white of his teeth, told her he spent a great deal of time outdoors.

Courtney flushed as he quickly lifted his head and caught her staring. Their eyes locked. Again a warm and intimate smile lighted his features as he calmly tossed the folder aside.

The frank admiration she saw in his level blue eyes put her on edge. She wanted to shout at him either to give her the contract outright or send her on her way. But she couldn't utter a word. All she could do was sit here and stare at this enigma of a man like some tongue-tied teenager.

Turning toward her once again, Kace said, "Miss Roberts, do you realize this is a big job that will demand long hours and hard, accurate work on your part?"

Courtney didn't hesitate. "I have complete confidence in my word processing service. I *assure* you my assistant and I will be able to handle any type of work no matter how difficult or detailed."

Kace's gaze raked her face warmly. "Well, there's no doubt," he drawled slowly, "that I'm impressed with your credentials."

Courtney moistened her lips nervously. With each passing second, the situation was becoming more complicated, more overpowering. Why on earth was she allowing his flirtatious innuendoes to set her on edge? In the past she had put men, both young and old, in their place for much less than he had gotten away with. Why then was she allowing Kace McCord to make her feel tense, threatened?

Refusing to linger on these troubling thoughts, Courtney forced herself to concentrate on what Kace was saying.

"First on the agenda will be the real estate paper work," his well-modulated voice intoned. "The latest condominiums I've built, I've decided to sell myself. Therefore, I've been forced to hire outside help. My secretary simply can't handle the extra work."

Courtney nodded. "I understand. I've just recently completed feeding into our word processor, pleadings and motions for the Johnston Realty Company. They were more than satisfied with my work."

"Good," he acknowledged. "That takes care of that. *But*, as soon as the real estate part is taken care of there'll be the public offerings, perspectives, financial statements, and numerous communication memos to contend with."

"I can take care of all of those too. No problem. Anything else?" Courtney squared her shoulders, daring him to question her capabilities any further.

He smiled. "I think that about covers it. For right now, anyway." He shut her folder and laid it aside.

Courtney found herself noting with fascination the way the hairs grew on the back of his hand and on the knuckles of his long fingers. Realizing what she was doing, she quickly averted her gaze. What was happening to her?

"Do you have any more questions?" Kace's quiet voice nudged her out of her musings.

She shook her head negatively and waited with bated breath for him to tell her that the job would be hers. There was more work involved than she had anticipated, but along with the extra work would come more money.

Instead Kace stood up and walked toward the coffee bar in the corner of his office. Turning toward her he asked, "How do you like your coffee, Miss Roberts?"

Courtney moved impatiently. "I don't care for any, thank you."

He half smiled. "You don't know what you're missing when you pass up my black brew."

Courtney heaved a sigh, suppressing a faint sense of uneasiness spiced with irritation. "I make it a point never to drink coffee after eight o'clock. It's bad for the digestive system."

He grinned, his eyes narrowing in laughter as he raised his cup to her in a mock salute.

Courtney felt more than a little disconcerted as his melting gaze lingered first on her slightly parted lips and then on the gentle rise and fall of her breasts. Coffee suddenly became the farthest thing from her mind. All she wanted was to get the contract and get away from those piercing blue eyes. The complications Kace McCord could cause in her life didn't even warrant pursuing. It was akin to throwing a lighted match in a can of gasoline.

"Will you have dinner with me this evening?" he asked abruptly.

Courtney stared at him incredulously. "What!" Realizing she was shouting, she lowered her voice. "I—I don't understand. You—you can't be serious." She felt her tongue cling to the roof of her dry mouth.

"Oh, but I am," Kace regarded her intently. "I never issue idle invitations."

Courtney swallowed hard. "What about the contract, Mr. McCord?"

"All in good time, Miss Roberts. All in good time," he stressed, amusement lacing his voice.

Courtney chewed her lower lip, stalling for time. What now? she asked herself. If she didn't accept his offer for dinner, she could very well scratch any chance of securing the contract. On the other hand, she had no desire to have anything to do with Kace McCord except on a purely business level. What was there about this man that could so easily put her on the defensive? Make her feel apprehensive?

Taking a deep breath, Courtney rose from her chair on rather shaky legs. She decided the best and only way to deal with a situation like this was to lay all the cards on the table. "Are you threatening me, Mr. McCord?" she asked, schooling her features to show none of the inner turmoil she was feeling.

Kace's eyes darkened. However, his voice was velvet smooth when he answered her. "Of course not. There are a few other points we need to discuss. What better way than over a chilled glass of wine and a good dinner?" He cocked his head to one side, his face completely devoid of all expression. "Don't you agree?"

His feigned innocence didn't fool her for one moment.

Courtney cautioned herself not to let him back her into a corner—contract or no contract. *If you give this man an inch,* she cautioned herself, *he'll take a mile!*

"Oh come on, Miss Roberts, it can't be as bad as all that, surely?" He paused, grinning. "If I promise not to bite, will you come?"

Courtney failed to see any humor in the situation. "Very well," she sighed in defeat. "However," she went on firmly, "I expect this to be a business dinner only."

Kace chuckled. "Anything you say. Will seven be all right?"

Courtney nodded. "I'll be ready, Mr. McCord." She was striving painfully to keep things on an even keel as she made her way toward the door. She grabbed the doorknob as if it were a lifeline.

"By the way, my name's Kace—Courtney."

The only sound in the room was the loud thumping of her heart. She opened her mouth to reply and then closed it.

Courtney didn't breathe until she was on the elevator plunging downward. She had to clutch the handrail to keep her knees from buckling under her.

She was moving as if in slow motion when she came out of the McCord Building in the business district of downtown New Orleans. Even the cool December breeze off Lake Pontchartrain failed to penetrate her befuddled senses. She was trembling as she maneuvered her car into the busy traffic. This will never do! she scolded herself as the loud honk of a horn forced her back into the proper lane. At this rate, she wouldn't make it back to her office in one piece.

After the near accident, Courtney forced herself to concentrate on her driving. The noon traffic was horrendous, and it required her full concentration to drive in it. With no more mishaps, she finally whipped her car off Canal Street onto a little side street at the outer edge of the French Quarter.

Parking her car in the tiny space allotted to her and Amy, Courtney quickly made her way into the quaint but compact office. She breathed a sign of relief on seeing she had the office to herself. Going quickly to what was referred to as the general "catchall" room, she grabbed a cola out of the small refrigerator and plopped down into the nearest chair.

She had to gather her scattered wits about her, she told herself, before Amy came breezing in demanding all the details concerning her meeting with Kace McCord. Courtney groaned aloud as the mere thought of that man's name could cause her palms to turn moist. Now that she had time to think, she was aware she had allowed him to sweet-talk her into going out to dinner with him with relative ease. She had been outwitted and outmaneuvered by Kace McCord, and she still couldn't believe she had allowed it to happen. Had experience taught her nothing?

Courtney's well-ordered life had suddenly been turned topsy-turvy, and she was at a loss as to how to cope.

"Where are you, Courtney?" Amy called, breaking into her thoughts with a jolt.

"I'm back here having a cold drink," she answered.

"Well, tell me, did we get the contract?" Excitement gushed from Amy Neal's voice as she stood in the doorway staring wide-eyed at Courtney.

Courtney raised troubled eyes and took in her assistant's animated face. Amy was petite with short, honey brown hair that shaped her head like a smooth cap. No one would classify her as beautiful, but her large brown eyes and clearly defined features, combined with her warm personality, made one like her immediately.

Taking in the downward turn of Courtney's mouth, Amy's face lost its brightness. "Oh no!" she wailed. "Don't tell me, you didn't get the contract."

Courtney sighed. "Well, not yet, anyway." She dreaded telling Amy about her exchange with Kace. For some reason, she felt exposed, vulnerable. She wasn't at all comfortable with that feeling but was totally unsuccessful at shaking it. And she hated to hear Amy say, "I told you so."

At Amy's questioning look, Courtney rushed to explain. "Actually I think, or at least I hope, we'll get the contract, but *he* wants to discuss it in more detail over dinner tonight."

Amy threw back her head and laughed. "I hate to say I told you so, but . . ." Her eyes danced mischievously.

Courtney's lips pursed. "It's really not funny, my friend. I'll have to agree with you, though, he is different." She looked away from the smug gleam she saw in Amy's eyes. "But I don't want to have anything to do with him except on a business level." Even now, his piercing blue eyes had the power to disturb her.

Amy's expression grew serious. "You really are upset, aren't you?"

Courtney shrugged her slim shoulders. "A little. I wanted Mr. McCord to give me the contract outright, but he chose not to." She paused, taking a sip of her drink. "Well, anyway you know how I hate to be kept hanging."

Amy sensed Courtney wasn't telling her all that had

transpired between the two of them. "Are you sure that's all that's bothering you?"

Courtney leaned her head back against the couch and closed her eyes. "Well, if you must know, Mr. Kace McCord came on a bit too strong to suit me."

Amy chuckled. "What happened, did he make a pass at you?"

Courtney's eyes flew open. "Of course not!" she stressed.

"Methinks the lady doth protest too much," teased Amy.

A semblance of a smile tugged at the corners of Courtney's mouth. "Okay, so he's a good-looking hunk, silver hair and all. So what? I'm sure he has more women than Carter has little pills." She shrugged. "Anyway, you know I'm not interested."

"I know you're not," sighed Amy, "but gossip has it that since his wife died he's broken many a heart. His latest 'friend' just happens to be Joan Stevens who works for the Davis Abstract Company. We did some work for them about six months ago. Remember?"

"Vaguely." Courtney shrugged. Kace McCord and his women were certainly no concern of hers, she told herself rationally. So why the catch in her throat? She was behaving completely out of character. She needed to get hold of her emotions.

Realizing Amy was saying something else, she shook her head as if to clear it and stared at Amy blankly.

Amy's eyes narrowed. "You didn't hear a word I said, did you, Courtney Roberts?"

Courtney grinned sheepishly. "As a matter of fact, I didn't. I'm sorry."

"It wasn't important anyway," confirmed Amy with a smile.

Changing the subject, Courtney said, "By the way, were you able to get that multiple mailing contract from the New Orleans Savings and Loan?"

"I surely was," Amy answered brightly.

"Good! Let's get to work then, shall we?"

For the next several hours, they worked on the new contract, feeding the information Amy had obtained into the word processor. Courtney kept both her mind and her hands busy, so she wouldn't have time to think about the upcoming evening.

But as she drove home from work that afternoon, she wondered again if the contract with McCord was really worth it.

Courtney entered her condominium with the sense of unease remaining with her. She went immediately to her bedroom, where she kicked off her shoes and threw herself across the bed. She was tired and wanted desperately to get out of the dinner date this evening. Was she frightened of Kace McCord? She had kept thoughts of him at bay while at the office, but now his blue eyes were haunting her once again.

Groaning, she rolled off the bed and made her way into the kitchen. Maybe a cup of coffee with hot milk would help calm her. As she prepared the mixture, she surveyed the compact but brightly decorated kitchen. The yellow and blue combination enhanced by the skylight conveyed the overall cheerfulness of her new home. The two bedrooms and two baths, plus the large den with the breakfast room adjacent were Courtney's pride and joy.

A small inheritance left to her by her mother three

years ago had enabled Courtney to buy the condominium. The remaining portion of the money she had used to open her business. Together, her home and her business represented the most important things in her life. Her only living relatives were two aunts and an uncle in Texas, whom she rarely visited. She missed her mother terribly at times, but being the strong-minded person she was she managed to put her sorrow in the right perspective.

Since the night Hal had so painfully severed her blind trust in men, she had built a wall around her heart. Only one day before they were to be married Hal had eloped with her roommate.

Of course, as the years passed, her attitude toward the opposite sex took a turn for the better, but she had never forgotten the heartbreak or the humiliation. Although she had dated a number of handsome men, none had even come close to breaking down her wall of reserve, until now. Until Kace McCord. And what made the situation more mind boggling was that he was at least fifteen years older than she.

Courtney sat down on the couch with her coffee, hoping to have a few quiet moments before she had to dress, but, to her utter dismay, she found she was too nervous to sit still. *Stop it!* she told herself sharply. Stop thinking about him. You're overreacting. After all, he's just a man. You can handle him.

After disposing of the contents of her cup into the sink, Courtney made her way into the bedroom.

Noticing the time on the clock radio, Courtney decided she had better hurry. As she stripped herself of her clothing, she surveyed her body in the full-length mirror on the back of the door. Even though she hated to admit it to herself, she knew her figure was almost perfectly proportioned. Her breasts were high and firm, followed by a small waist, narrow hips, and long firm legs. She gave the credit for her supple body to her two-mile jog each morning. She felt she owed it to herself to keep her body in the very best of shape. It helped to maintain her self-confidence in meeting the public every day.

It was her job to call on prospective clients to solicit work for Paper-Work-Plus. She had earned the reputation for being brilliant at her work and was highly respected. The McCord Builders' contract would be the icing on the cake, so to speak. It was the boost her business needed to put her into the solid financial ranks.

Leaving the bedroom, she dashed off to the shower. The brisk cold water helped to get her tired muscles moving. After carefully applying her makeup, she opened her closet and closely scrutinized its contents.

She decided to wear a burgundy-colored dress of soft wool, styled for a soft blouson effect, with an easy-fitting elasticized waist. Courtney stepped into it and acknowledged without conceit that its color complemented her dark hair and fair creamy skin.

She was spraying herself with her favorite perfume when the soft peal of the doorbell halted her actions. She sat the perfume bottle down with shaking hands. Taking a deep breath, she quickly took another look at her overall appearance before making her way out of the room.

She opened the door to a smiling Kace McCord. Courtney caught her breath as she took in his ruddy good looks. He was impeccably dressed in a tailored dark blue suit. Gone were the khakis and the worn boots. A crisp white shirt collar met the tapered length of his silver hair. His blue eyes were equally appreciative as he took in the stunning picture she made. His eyes seemed to devour her.

Courtney's stomach lurched dizzily as she murmured, "Hello. Please come in."

Kace stepped into the softly lighted den and looked about him with interest, approving of the decor. Its modern brightness combined with the cozy warmth made one feel instantly at home.

"You've got a nice place here. I like it." His gaze rested on her face, warm and tender.

"I'm—I'm glad," she stammered. Courtney was appalled at her actions. Why, she wondered, did she react so strongly to this man? It was going to be a long evening.

"Are you ready?" A slow heartrending smile curved his lips.

"Yes, I'm ready," she murmured. She quickly checked the contents of her purse, making sure she had her keys.

They went the short distance to the car in silence. The late December evening was chilly, but not uncomfortably so. The shiver that penetrated Courtney's body wasn't from the cold but from the strong fingers that gripped her arm. He didn't turn her loose until he had carefully seated her in his silver Mercedes.

She was still smiling as he seated himself behind the steering wheel, adjusting himself behind the seat to accommodate his large frame. He paused to look at her. "Care to share the joke with me?" he asked softly.

"It's nothing really," she said, flushing. "I just noticed that your car is the same color as your hair."

He laughed. "So it is." His voice was warmly teasing. "Do you like it?"

"Which one, your hair or your car?" she quipped.

"Both," he countered, his blue eyes twinkling.

"Yes to both," she laughed, before averting her eyes.

"I'm glad," he stated. His grin broadened as he switched on the ignition.

They drove south toward the French Quarter. Courtney was lost in her own thoughts as she took in the Christmas decorations that still lined the streets. Although the religious holiday had come and gone, many people left their decorations up until New Year's, which was still three days away. Although she had enjoyed the holiday, it wasn't the same now that her mother was gone. She spent Christmas Day with Amy and her family, but the inner loneliness remained with her. And New Year's Eve was no different. She preferred to spend it at home. Boisterous parties were no longer of interest to her. The invitations had ceased coming a long time ago.

"I hope Brennans is all right with you?" Kace remarked, breaking sharply into her thoughts. "I don't think you can beat their stuffed flounder anywhere in New Orleans."

Courtney forced a faint smile. "It doesn't matter to me where we go, just as long as we can discuss business there." She had to put the evening back into the right perspective. Food and intimate conversation wasn't her goal—but getting that contract was!

"Oh, I think we can manage, don't you?" he drawled softly.

Courtney tightened her lips at the veiled teasing she heard in his voice. What kind of game was he playing? she wondered despairingly. She was beginning to have her doubts that the contract would even be discussed.

Kace leaned over abruptly and squeezed the hand nearest him. "Relax," he demanded. "I want you to enjoy yourself."

Courtney's heart slammed up to her throat as the touch of his roughened hand sent electric currents shooting through her body. Shocked by the intensity of her reaction to him, she turned her head away to hide her embarrassment.

Kace parked the car on Iberville Street, just inside the French Quarter, and they walked the short distance to the restaurant. The sounds of New Orleans filled the night air around them.

Brennans was one of the city's finest restaurants and a real favorite of Courtney's. Although she didn't dine here often, she took advantage of every chance she did get. They were escorted to the softly lit bar, where they were seated while a table was being prepared. There was another heavy silence between them as they sipped their before-dinner drinks in a leisurely fashion.

It wasn't until they were comfortably seated at their table that Kace turned the conversation toward business.

"I want you to meet with my lawyer around noon tomorrow. Is that agreeable?"

Courtney could barely contain her excitement. "Are you telling me I'm going to get the contract?" She held her breath waiting for his answer.

A smile hovered near the corner of his mouth. "Were you ever really in doubt, Courtney?"

"Of course I was in doubt," she answered more sharply than she intended.

"Well, you shouldn't have been," he admonished.

She inclined her head. "I appreciate your confidence,"

she added breathlessly. "I plan to work days, evenings, and nights if I have to."

He frowned and looked seriously into her face. "I'm sorry, but I can't allow you to work evenings or nights."

Courtney stared at him dumbfounded.

"From now on," he went on calmly, "your evenings and nights belong exclusively to me."

2

Shock wrapped its tentacles tightly around Courtney as she sat frozen to the chair. For a timeless moment, speech escaped her. Was he the crazy one? she asked herself, or was she for sitting here listening to this man stake a claim on her life, her time. Absurd! That's what it was, absurd! Anger surged through her.

"Surely you're not surprised, honey?" he stated huskily. "You *know* something happened between us the first time we met. And don't try to deny it, either."

Courtney tossed her head back defiantly. "Oh, yes, I will too deny it!" she said tersely. She glanced around to make sure no one else had heard her rather loud outburst. "Granted, I wanted your business, but that's all, Mr. McCord. Believe it or not, I'm perfectly satisfied with my life the way it is. I don't need a man to complicate things."

His only reaction to her heated words was to lift one eyebrow. "I don't know why you insist on fighting this thing between us, but I'm warning you right now—it won't do any good. I'll never give up!" He paused significantly. "And one more time, my name is Kace," he added in a tone of deadly calm.

Courtney shook her head as if to clear it. She couldn't believe this was happening to her. It was all so ridiculous! She should have followed her instinct and canceled this dinner date no matter what!.

Silence descended over the table as the waiter approached. With ease, Kace ordered the house specialty for both of them. It didn't make any difference to Courtney what she was served. The thought of food turned her stomach.

After the waiter disappeared, she kept her eyes glued to the candle in the middle of the table. She was trying desperately to marshal her defenses and launch a counterattack. But when she looked up her eyes locked with Kace's. She suddenly felt she was drowning.

He was watching her with a gentle scrutiny. There was no smugness or cockiness in his expression, only genuine interest and concern.

"I'd like to get my hands on the guy who's responsible for putting that look of fear in your eyes," he said conversationally.

Courtney felt her face drain of every ounce of color at his personal remark. Don't say or do anything foolish, she told herself. Just keep a cool head. The evening couldn't last forever, could it?

She pressed her lips firmly together, saying nothing. The silence stretched.

"Relax," he murmured. "I'm not about to hurt a hair

on your beautiful head. I just want you to know where I stand, that's all." His voice was low-pitched, caressing.

"Please . . ." she began, only to have words fail her. What more could she say? Kace McCord was like a bulldozer—determined and aggressive. Her hands were twined around her glass. She couldn't allow him to see how badly they were shaking.

To her surprise, he reached over and uncurled a hand from around the glass. He carried it to his lips, turning it over and kissing her palm with warm insistence before releasing it.

Courtney's insides melted. Was there to be no end to this torment? Here she sat like a statue, mesmerized by this man's touch, his eyes, his silver hair. Where was her fighting sprit? Shouldn't she be up and gone, flagging down a taxi to take her home?

"Ah, here comes our food," Kace noted, his voice relaxed. His eyes, as they swung around to face her, were once again tender. He watched her closely as the waiter quietly and unobtrusively served their food and then retreated.

She gave him a withering look, which only made him grin crookedly.

"Temper, temper," he whispered calmly, as he leaned toward her. "It doesn't become you."

"If you don't quit treating me like a dimwitted child," she retaliated through clenched teeth, "I'm going to get up right this minute and walk out of here!" Her green eyes were flashing fire.

Laughter shone from his eyes. "All right," he agreed, although obviously not repentant. "I promise I won't say another word about our relationship until after we've eaten. I want you to enjoy your meal."

"For some reason, I seem to have lost my appetite," she returned sarcastically.

Kace shrugged lightly and smiled. "You'll get it back after you bite into this delicious flounder. Mmm . . . it's good."

Didn't anything penetrate his shell of conceit? she wondered. He was unbelievable! And her reaction to him was unbelievable! It was as if he had cast a spell upon her. Courtney was aware of the other people in the room—there was the usual amount of clamor and clatter associated with any restaurant—but it all seemed to go completely beyond her. It seemed as though she were all alone in this room with him!

After heartily consuming his food, Kace leaned his broad shoulders back in his chair and watched Courtney pick at her food. "The quicker you eat, the sooner we can get out of here," he told her pointedly.

Silence followed his words, and Courtney could feel his speculative regard and his silent deliberation.

She managed to take a few bites of the rich flounder, only to lay her fork down quickly as the sudden lurch of her stomach warned her: no more.

Shortly thereafter, Courtney found herself being escorted out of the restaurant into the refreshing night air. She breathed deeply, trying to clear her senses.

But uneasiness snaked its way through her as Kace casually draped his arm around her shoulders. His touch sent a shudder through her—it was all consuming. From somewhere deep within, she told herself, she must find the strength to fight him.

As she pulled away from the heat of his body, she quickened her steps. She chose to ignore his warm chuckle as it echoed through the night air.

"There's no escape, you know," he remarked softly, matching her hasty stride, step for step.

Although he was no longer touching her, Courtney was intensely aware of him. She expelled a sigh of relief as she soon found herself in the car and headed toward home. She was annoyed as well as confused by her potent reaction to Kace. She had no intention of seeing him after tonight. And if getting the contract meant working with him on a one-to-one basis, then she would have to forfeit the contract. Amy would just have to understand.

They were parked in her driveway before she realized it. In a fluid motion, Kace leaned across the seat and pulled her gently against his muscled chest. She could smell the clean, male frangrance of him: the musk odor of his cologne made her senses spin. Her heart began thudding erratically as their eyes met and held. The silence was uncanny as the moonlight danced around them. He slowly lifted the mass of silky hair and began nibbling and kissing the side of her neck.

"Please," Courtney whispered, her voice strangled. "You, you, promised you wouldn't . . ."

"I lied," Kace murmured warmly.

"Ohhh, you . . . you," Courtney spluttered. She then tried to push him away, but the effort was fruitless. It was too late. She could smell his warm breath as his lips slowly claimed hers. She almost stopped breathing. It was a yearning, hungry kiss whose forceful intensity seemed to draw her very soul from her.

When he finally withdrew his lips, she felt his gaze linger, drinking in the sweetness of her face. Courtney sat there motionless for a long paralyzed moment. She felt perspiration dampen her palms as she locked her hands tightly in her lap. She refused to look at him, unable to believe what had just happened.

She was shaken to the depths of her being as an uncontrollable tremor started somewhere deep within her. What now? she asked herself. He was probably thinking he had her exactly where he wanted her. Well, she would just have to prove him wrong. True, her control had slipped this one time—but not again. Tomorrow she would don her cloak of professionalism and self-control and remove all trace of Mr. Kace McCord from her life. Having reassured herself of her position, she felt able to cope with the situation.

The husky timbre of Kace's voice broke sharply into her troubled thoughts. "This is just the beginning of what I have planned for you—for us." He paused, with a sigh. "Since my wife died, I've never found anyone that I cared to see more than once or twice." His voice deepened with desire. "You're so young, so fresh, so beautiful. . . . But more important, you've filled a void in my life."

"Please—please—don't. Don't say things like that to me," she told him urgently. "You, you don't have the right."

His laugh was low and intimate. "We'll see. But right now, I'd better go and let you get some sleep." He paused, significantly. "We," he stressed, "have a lot to take care of tomorrow."

Too bemused and tired to argue any further, Courtney sat stoically while Kace came around the car and opened the door for her. As soon as the key was in the lock, Kace took his leave, but not before he planted a swift hard kiss on her lips. Finding herself alone at last, she leaned against the door and breathed a shaky sigh of relief. She refused to think beyond shedding her clothes and getting into bed. Her brain was too scrambled to do otherwise.

Sleep, however, eluded her. She rolled and tumbled until she was exhausted, but sleep still did not come. Her thoughts jumped from Kace's face and passionate words to that fateful night eight years ago when she had gone to Hal's apartment. . . .

With only two days left before she and Hal were to have been married, they had spent the evening at his apartment. His lovemaking had been much more aggressive and demanding than usual. He had tried desperately to make love to her. But, as always, she had managed to stop him short of final consummation with the age-old excuse that she wanted to march down the aisle a virgin. However, that time a bitter quarrel had followed with them parting less than amicably.

Later, after considerable thought, she decided she had been unreasonable and prudish in making him wait. After all, she told herself, they were to be married in less than two days, anyway. So the next night she had gone to his apartment to make amends. She used the extra key to let herself in. She knew Hal was on a photography assignment and would be working late. She planned to cook his dinner and surprise him.

But Courtney was the one who was surprised. What happened after she stepped into that apartment was still as clear in her mind now as it was then.

She first noticed the empty wine bottle on the coffee table. Then, to further convince her that all was not as it should have been, there were the cigarette butts in a nearby ashtray; Hal didn't smoke. As she ventured farther into the apartment she looked around quickly, but saw nothing else amiss. Then she went to the bedroom and peered in. For a moment she thought Hal hadn't gone to work. His head was dark on the pillow. But as the body on the bed groaned and moved, the covers had shifted, and a woman's naked shoulder appeared out from under the sheet.

Courtney stood there, feeling as though her insides had been kicked out. Clutching for breath, she whirled and, with tears blinding her eyes, bounded out of the apartment.

The next day a letter was waiting for her. With a sick feeling in the pit of her stomach, she ripped it open. Hal explained that it was destiny that had thrown him and Marilyn together, and they planned to be married immediately. He went on to inform Courtney that he had taken a job out of the country and by the time she read the letter they would be on their way there.

His next words, "Use your own discretion concerning the wedding presents, the church, etc. In time I hope you'll forgive me. Don't blame Marilyn. It's all my fault" had become words that she despaired of ever forgetting.

Even now, lying in bed, she broke into a cold sweat. She let the humiliation, the anger, the embarrassment, and the wounded pride wash over her once again. And all because of a glib-tongued, silver-haired devil, too! In a short period of time, he had aroused feelings in her that she had thought permanently dormant. The attraction was there, yes. She'd be a fool not to admit it. But she wasn't about to let herself become involved with a man too old for her, or one that took romantic entanglements so lightly.

She could just chalk up the moments in his arms

tonight to temporary madness. Punching her pillow in self-derision, she promised herself there would not be a repeat of this evening. With this thought uppermost in her mind, she finally drifted into a deep sleep.

If it hadn't been for the sunlight filtering through the mini-blinds, Courtney surmised she would have slept the entire morning away. Groaning, she rolled over and shut off the offensive buzz of the alarm clock. Noticing that it was nine-thirty, she made a conscious effort to get out of bed.

Before she could make good her intentions, however, the phone beside her bed began ringing shrilly. For a fraction of a second, her heart took a dive, then settled back to normal when she realized it was probably Amy wondering where she was.

On about the fifth ring, she lifted the receiver. "Hello," she murmured, hesitantly.

"Good morning, sleepyhead," the velvet-edged voice caressed warmly.

Silence.

"Courtney?"

"Yes."

He laughed.

Courtney gripped the receiver so tightly she cut off the circulation in her hand.

"Were you asleep?" he asked huskily.

She refused to be drawn into conversational small talk. "What do you want?" she demanded. "Why are you calling me?" She hurled the words at him.

"Calm down, honey," he advised. "Didn't I warn you last night of my intentions?"

"Please . . ."

Kace broke in abruptly. "I'll pick you up at your office at one-thirty. We'll have lunch with my lawyer and discuss business. Bye for now, honey."

Courtney sat holding the receiver for a long moment, the dial tone sounding loud and clear in her ear. Mechanically she made herself get up and get dressed. Her thoughts were in a turmoil. Her decision of last evening to be firm and self-assured died when she heard his voice on the phone. What should she do? How could she handle Kace McCord? How could she put him in his place once and for all? It would be so much easier if he wasn't so calm, cool, and collected. And so positive. How did one combat those forces?

Sighing, she padded into the bathroom. A quick shower revived fogged senses, but not enough to make her go to any extra trouble making up her face or being choosy about what she wore. It was an hour later when she opened the door of her office.

"Where have you been?" Amy demanded. "I was just getting ready to pick up the phone and call you."

"I didn't hear my alarm," Courtney admitted sheepishly. "If it hadn't been for the sunlight, I'd probably still be sleeping." She purposely refrained from mentioning the phone call.

"Have a late night?" Amy questioned casually, too casually. She eyed her friend intently, taking in the dark smudges under her eyes and the tired droop of her shoulders.

Courtney crossed the room to the coffee pot. "I wasn't out all that late, actually." She paused to pour herself a cup of the scalding liquid. "But it was early this morning before I finally slept."

"Well, did we or didn't we?"

Courtney blinked her eyes, looking puzzled. Then it dawned on her. "The contract? You want to know about the contract." Her mouth curved downward. "It's ours if we want it. But," she went on hurriedly, "I'm going to turn it down."

Amy looked horrified. "What!" she exclaimed. "But . . . but, I . . . I . . . Have you lost your mind?" she finally managed to stammer.

Courtney held up her hand, cutting off her assistant's tirade. "I know how we've been counting on it financially, but working for or with Kace McCord is absolutely impossible."

"What do you mean, impossible? What did he do—try to proposition you?"

Courtney flushed at Amy's astuteness. "Not exactly, but he won't take 'no' for an answer." She shook her head. "He's the most determined man I've ever met. Maybe bull-headed is a better word for him," she finished forcefully.

Amy grinned. "I'll take my hat off to any man who can break through that wall you've built around yourself."

"I hate to disappoint you," Courtney said, flashing Amy a hard look, "but I'm not about to let myself develop an interest in a known ladies' man like Kace McCord!"

Amy shrugged. "It's up to you, of course, whether you want to date McCord or not, but I hate to see you let this good opportunity slip through your fingers because of your animosity toward him."

"Oh, Amy," Courtney wailed, "you just don't understand." Her voice broke. And she hated herself for this show of weakness, even if it was in front of her best friend.

Amy looked at her sympathetically. "I understand more than you give me credit for. You're attracted to him, and you despise yourself for it. Right?"

Courtney nodded, her voice too full to speak.

"If I promised to handle all the communication with Mr. McCord, would you reconsider and accept the contract?"

Courtney heaved a sigh. "I don't know. . . ." Uncertainty laced her voice.

"It'll work, I know it will," Amy replied enthusiastically. She began pacing the floor. "Once we get the initial agreement worked out satisfactorily, the work itself will be a piece of cake."

Courtney's mouth curved wryly. "You're probably right about that aspect of it, but there's already a complication."

"What?" Amy asked sharply, pausing in her tracks.

"He—he called this morning and is determined to pick me up here at the office and from here go to a business lunch with his lawyer."

"Do you think he'd object if I went instead of you?" Amy inquired, quirking her eyebrow.

Courtney's smile didn't quite reach her eyes. "Oh, he'll object, all right. But I think he's too much of a gentleman to come right out and tell you that you can't go."

Amy's eyes narrowed. "So, does that mean you're willing to try it?"

"Only if you are." But already Courtney's features were less drawn.

"Sure, why not," Amy shrugged. "I'll do anything to

get that contract." She grinned. "Well, almost anything, that is. It beats me how you or anyone else could ever pass up the chance to be around that eligible hunk." Her eyes were teasing.

Courtney laughed. "You're crazy, you know that. But I'm game, if you are. It'll certainly be worth a try."

"Good," Amy replied. "Then why don't you go call on a couple of clients, and when he comes knocking, he'll be forced to settle for little ole me." She grinned impishly.

The next two hours were spent working. While Amy sat at the word processor, Courtney made several phone calls and posted the monthly expenses in the ledger. Although the business was solvent, the McCord contract would certainly be an added boost. She must keep up front in her mind, however, that other good opportunities would come along—if this one failed to work out.

Courtney didn't need to look at her watch to know it was past lunch time. She usually ate at twelve o'clock, hence the rumble of her stomach told her food was long overdue and Kace's arrival was close. She planned to leave the office no later than one o'clock. That way she would be gone at least thirty minutes before Kace was due to arrive. She couldn't help but smile to herself when she thought about how furious he would be on learning he had been duped. It was no less than he deserved, she thought smugly.

After hurriedly repairing her makeup, she wished Amy good luck, adding a conspiratorial wink, and stepped out into the cloudy winter day. She took a deep breath, taking in the sights and sounds of the French Quarter. A native of New Orleans, Courtney couldn't imagine living anywhere else. She loved the excitement and unpredictability of this city.

Courtney lowered her head, buttoning her camel-colored blazer to break the chill of the wind. She didn't see the silver Mercedes parked by the curb. Just as she was about to pass by it, the door swung open blocking her path.

"Going somewhere, honey?" Kace asked in a casual drawl.

Courtney halted in her tracks. The honey-toned voice caused her stomach to turn upside down. Quickly raising her head, she feasted her eyes on Kace's beautiful and powerful body as he slowly climbed out of the car. He was dressed in a pair of navy corduroy pants and light blue sweater—the exact color of his eyes, she noted.

When their eyes met, they locked in open warfare.

Kace was the first to speak. "You didn't really think you'd get away with running out on me, now did you?" Although his tone was now velvet smooth, Courtney wasn't fooled. He was extremely provoked at her for attempting to avoid their meeting.

Her thoughts darted wildly as she pulled her eyes away from his frosty blue ones. Oh damn, damn, damn! Why did he have the power to make her feel like a child caught with her hand in the cookie jar? Or better yet, like a trapped animal? She should have realized that she couldn't get the better of him.

He seemed to know the raging battle that was taking place inside of her, but his eyes showed little signs of softening as he said brusquely, "Please, get in."

Stiff-lipped, Courtney whipped around and lowered herself into the car's plush interior. It was either acquiesce or create a scene. With a firm slam of the door, Kace made his way around the car and eased himself behind the wheel. Within seconds, they were battling the lunch-time traffic.

Frustration engulfed her as she stared straight ahead, refusing to look in his direction. Courtney knew she was displaying her temper, but she didn't like being backed into a corner. Why couldn't he take the hint and leave her alone?

"How long are you going to pout?" Kace prodded gently.

Color flowered in her cheeks as she swung around to face him. She was flabbergasted and showed it. It was about time she put him in his place, she decided.

Laughter glimmered in his eyes as he took in her mutinous expression. "Did anyone ever tell you how gorgeous you are when you're mad?"

Courtney felt herself bristle for a moment and then, realizing how she must appear to him, expelled her pent-up breath slowly. All he had to do was open his mouth, and she was up in arms like a prim old-fashioned schoolmarm. She was twenty-nine and acting like twenty-one. Where was her self-discipline? Her sense of humor? Her self-control? There was only one way to get the better of this man, and that was to beat him at his own game.

So, in her most business-like tone, Courtney said, "Please, Kace, I'd like to go back to the office." She sighed. "It's obviously no secret now that I hadn't planned to keep our appointment." She paused, wetting her lips nervously. "Amy, my assistant, was supposed to go in my place," she added in a rush.

"I see," he commented lightly. Too lightly.

Courtney hesitated. "To be perfectly honest, I want the

contract, but I don't want to have to see you on a daily basis to get it." She held her breath waiting for the explosion. When it didn't come, she ventured a hesitant glance in his direction.

Although he said nothing, his features told the story. They were withdrawn and unyielding as he busied himself parking the car.

Well, Courtney told herself with an inward sigh, I've done it now. I've finally made him mad. He'll take me back to the office, and it'll all be over.

Shoving the car into park, Kace turned to face her. His eyes were dark and unreadable. "I realize I ought to be upset with you for your childish stunt." He chose to ignore Courtney's gasp. "But I know you haven't as yet come to terms with what's between us, so, I'm going to overlook it and pretend it never happened."

A cold shudder zipped through Courtney. "Now you listen to me, Kace McCord! I—"

"Didn't anyone ever tell you that you also talk too much?" he interrupted savagely. His words served to camouflage his actions. Before Courtney knew what was happening, she was locked securely in his arms. Wasting no time, Kace's head swooped down, and his lips fastened on hers and clung. Taking advantage of her parted lips, his tongue slowly, reverently began to explore the inner sweetness of her mouth.

Courtney found herself clinging wildly to the front of his sweater. Her mind was in a whirl. She couldn't believe she was actually involving herself in a replay of yesterday. But when he touched her like this she seemed to lose complete control of her emotions and her identity.

She could feel the hard muscular strength of his arms

and chest as his kiss plundered deeper, driving her head back against the soft seat. She moaned as a burning sensation flickered throughout her entire body. This feeling sent a sudden shaft of alarm coursing through her. As a result, she immediately withdrew her arms from around his neck and tried to put space between them.

"Kace, don't . . ." she pleaded against his lips. In the distance, she could hear the loud honk of a horn and the swish of traffic. As it dawned upon her where they were, flags of color stained her cheeks. She renewed her efforts to break away from him.

With a warm chuckle vibrating in her ear, Courtney found herself once more on her side of the car—alone. She turned toward him, her utter dismay mirrored on her face. "I, I can't believe this. . . . I can't believe you. . . . I feel like I've just given the public a free show!"

She knew she was muttering, not making any sense. But she found it hard to accept that she, Courtney Roberts, was sitting in a parking lot in downtown New Orleans carrying on with a man she had known only two days! It was all so absurd! Crazy!

His soft teasing voice cut into her scuttling thoughts. "I have to admit this isn't my idea of the perfect place to make love to you." He paused, holding her gaze. "I only hope I'm not destined to carry out my whole plan of seduction in the front seat of a car." Laughter glimmered in his eyes. "Now what I really have in mind is a king-size bed, no clothes, our bodies moving together in perfect harmony. And . . ."

Courtney raised her hands in one swift motion to cover her ears. "Stop!" she demanded. "Don't say another word!" His words caused a tingling feeling to zigzag up and down her spine. She couldn't bear to think about the images that his words conjured up.

Kace was grinning openly now, but there was an unfamiliar darkness in his eyes. Courtney knew a certain gravity underlined his words.

She opened her mouth to speak only to close it abruptly. What was the use? she fumed to herself. This man couldn't be for real, could he? And she couldn't continue to let him manipulate her life like this and get away with it, could she?

While these chaotic thoughts ran rampant through her mind, Kace had come around the car and was holding the door open for her. He stood there eyeing her intently.

"Are you coming?" he asked easily, although with a hint of challenge in his voice.

Courtney, her lips tight, slid out of the car, ignoring his outstretched hand. As she stood up, she felt light-headed, off balance. She was confused, embarrassed, and angry with herself for her own lack of restraint. What was happening to her? she wondered for what seemed like the thousandth time. It was as if she was on a roller coaster with no brakes—a collision inevitable.

With tension coiled tightly within her, Courtney found herself being escorted into an informal but quaint soup and sandwich shop. She barely had time to notice her surroundings before she and Kace were being led to a quiet table in the rear. As they approached the table, a young man with hair the exact shade of copper arose. He smiled, extending his hand first to Kace and then to Courtney.

"Hello," he said enthusiastically, a broad smile covering his entire face. "I'm Mark Davidson. You're Courtney, I take it."

"Right," she agreed, withdrawing her hand after he shook it heartily.

"Well, we're glad to have you aboard. Aren't we, Kace?" Although he addressed his boss, his eyes didn't move an inch from Courtney's tall graceful body.

"You betcha," Kace returned roundly.

Courtney acknowledged their compliment with a smile but refrained from commenting.

As Kace pulled out a chair, carefully seating her, Courtney rested her gaze on Kace's friend and lawyer. He seemed harmless enough, although his freckles and scrubbed little-boy look could very well be misleading. She would reserve judgment until later, she told herself.

The waiter appeared to take their orders. Afterward the conversation turned to business. For the next two hours, Courtney found herself deeply involved in the details of the work Kace wanted her firm, Paper-Work-Plus, to handle. She wouldn't be human if she didn't feel excitement at the challenge that was being offered her. And the money! The amount Kace quoted to her was staggering! There was no way she could pass it up. Only a fool would do that. And in spite of her faults, she was no fool. Anyway, if she did refuse, Amy would certainly have her head. But, she promised herself, someway, somehow, she would find a way for Amy to work with Kace. Mark she could handle. But Kace, no way. With this meeting, their volatile relationship must come to an end.

Halfway back to her office, a short time later, Courtney turned toward Kace. "You can wipe that smug look off your face," she remarked briskly. "Just because . . ."

Kace threw back his head and laughed outright, interrupting her in mid-sentence. "Have I told you lately,

Courtney Roberts, that you're the delight of my life. And that I can't wait to take you under my wing and teach you how to laugh and to love?"

A half-smile curved her lips in spite of her efforts to remain aloof, but she replied somewhat sarcastically. "No, as a matter of fact, you haven't used that line before."

"Ah, ah," he exclaimed in mock severity, "I must be slipping. I could have sworn I'd said that to you." His eyes twinkled. "I guess I'll have to do better."

Courtney's pulse raced at these intimate word games. She should be repulsed by the things he said to her, but she wasn't. If she continued to play with fire, she told herself, she would deserve to get burned.

"Snap out of it, honey." Kace's honey-toned voice cut sharply into her introspection. "You didn't hear one word I said to you, did you?"

She shook her head negatively.

"Okay, I'll repeat it, then," he announced indulgently. "I said I'll be out of town for a couple of days. But I'll be back in time to take you to the Sugar Bowl game and out to dinner."

3

~oococceocooo~

This man certainly had the talent for rendering her speechless. Here he was assuming she would go out with him again.

Swallowing her irritation, Courtney said, in what she hoped was a cool voice, "I'm sorry, but I already have plans for New Year's Day."

"Break them," Kace ordered mildly.

Courtney's eyes widened. "I most certainly will not!"

"Break them," he repeated. This time his voice was edged with steel.

Courtney noticed they were now parked in front of her office; she was tempted to jump out of the car and run without a backward glance. But she knew any move on her part would only be in vain. Kace was more than capable of stopping her. Creating a scene wouldn't bother him in the least, especially if it meant getting what he wanted. And he made it quite plain that he wanted her, Courtney.

"Why are you frightened of me?" Kace asked softly in rebuttal to her stiff-lipped silence.

Courtney bent her head, her silky curls hiding her face. "Oh, but I'm not . . ." she began defiantly.

A thumb and forefinger reached over and captured her chin to turn it toward him. His touch effectively silenced her even before Kace rubbed his thumb across her lips.

"Oh, but you are," he told her softly as he reluctantly withdrew his hand. "You have absolutely no reason to feel that way either." His eyes probed hers, and she could feel herself getting hot all over. "If I take it slow and easy, will you let me take you out and show you a good time?" He sighed deeply. "I promise I won't do anything you don't want me to."

"I don't . . ."

"Tell you what," he cut in briskly, "I'll call you the minute I get back into town, and we'll finalize the plans then." Without giving her a chance to respond, much to her chagrin, he pushed open the door. His arm gently grazed her breast. "Out with you now," he murmured huskily, "or you'll play hell getting out of here at all! I've got a plane to catch."

Courtney was finding it difficult to breathe, much less move. Even with his high-handed manner, she was rendered motionless. The touch of his hand to her breast, light though it was, both confused and annoyed her. It just wasn't fair, she fumed, that his touch could play such havoc with her emotions.

"Honey, I'm warning you," came Kace's husky reminder.

Those words served to penetrate Courtney's bewildered senses. Swiftly she was out the door and into her office before she realized it.

On shaky legs, she made it to her desk and fell into the chair. Propping her elbows on the desk and cupping her chin in her hands, she stared into space. Would she be making a mistake by agreeing to spend a day and evening in his company?

What could she hope to accomplish by doing so? She had to admit that Kace was perhaps the most exciting and charming man she'd ever met. Besides being the most handsome. But she didn't want to become involved. Anyway, Kace, according to Amy, wasn't content to remain with the same woman for long. So what would be the point in going with him? She was still holding firm to her conviction to never be at the mercy of any man again, even if that man had the power to set her pulses racing.

At the back of her mind, however, was the nagging assurance that Kace could and would create a good deal of misery for her if she refused him. *No* was a word that didn't seem to be a part of his vocabulary. So, after a little more soul searching, she decided she may as well go. One last time.

The next two and a half days passed in a whirl for Courtney. When she wasn't at the office plowing through the McCord contracts, she was cleaning her condominium, repotting plants, and otherwise keeping herself busy. When thoughts of Kace began to occupy her mind, she slipped into her running shoes and hit the jogging path. Running had always been her way of getting rid of all her pent-up emotions and nervous energy. She always felt like a new woman after she completed her two-mile trek. Today was no different.

Earlier this morning, she had run an extra mile, so she

was more than a little exhausted. She was expecting a call from Kace any minute now, as she had no idea what time he planned to come for her. It was a beautiful fall day, perfect for a football game, and she found herself looking forward to the outing, in spite of the misgivings she still harbored.

Courtney climbed out of the shower just in time to hear the sharp peal of the telephone. Grabbing a towel off the rack, she wrapped it around her and raced into the bedroom.

"Hello," she gasped, her breath coming in short spurts.

"Where were you?" Kace asked in his honey-toned voice. It had its usual effect on her. She felt her knees threaten to buckle at the possessive sweetness she heard there.

Courtney wet her lips nervously. "I—I—er—I was in the shower."

There was a deep silence.

"Kace, are you still there?" she asked hesitantly.

"Yes," he whispered intimately, "but I'd much rather be there with you instead."

"Kace, don't—you promised."

"All right, honey. I'm sorry," he sighed. "Just chalk it up to a slip of the tongue. But remember, I haven't seen you in almost three days," he added huskily.

"And whose fault is that?" she returned saucily.

"Don't push your luck, Courtney Roberts," he warned. But she could hear the laughter in his voice.

Courtney felt a flush creep into her cheeks at her audacity.

"I've made reservations at the Commander's Palace for six o'clock. How does that suit you?"

"Fine, I'll see you then."

After she hung up, Courtney hurried to get ready. By the time six o'clock rolled around, she was a bundle of nerves. She was dressed simply and casually in a soft wool skirt and sweater. The raspberry color was a perfect contrast for her blue-black hair. Her feet were daintily clad in low-heeled Italian sandals.

When she opened the door to admit Kace, he ran his eyes appreciatively over her figure. Smiling, he reached for her and planted a firm kiss on her parted lips.

"I've missed you," he assured her as his eyes took in every detail of her face. "And if we don't leave now, I'll be hard pressed to keep my promise not to molest you on sight." His eyes sparkled mischievously. Courtney felt laughter bubble within her. Yes, she was glad she had agreed to this one outing, she told herself. Kace McCord, with his infectious personality, would be good for her —if she continued to keep things in their right perspective.

They drove toward the uptown Garden District to Washington Avenue. Commander's Palace was a restored 1880s mansion and gardens that had been turned into a restaurant. The interior was filled with lush plants, and the furniture was all wicker.

After being shown to their table upstairs in the garden room, they ordered drinks and the special for dinner.

"Now," Kace said, positioning himself more comfortably in his chair, "I want to know everything there is to know about you."

"Everything?" Courtney laughed. "I can't imagine anything more boring."

Kace moved his arm to let the waiter place their drinks on the table. "I find that hard to believe," he commented lightly. "As far as I'm concerned, nothing you could do or say would ever bore me."

A feathering of goose bumps rippled Courtney's flesh at the intimacy of his tone and his look. She circled her dry lips with her tongue as she wondered what he was thinking when he looked at her like that. She was trying hard to conjure up something exciting to divulge about her life.

The moist tip of her tongue peeking through her lips was almost Kace's undoing. No woman had ever captivated him on first sight as this one had done. Each time she laughed or moved her lithesome body, he could see the tantalizing allure of her nipples silhouetted against the fabric of her clothing. He ached to hold her full breasts in his hand, to taste their sweetness. My God! How was he going to get through the entire evening without touching her? This was not the time for such thoughts, he told himself; but his body found it difficult to respond to common sense.

The sound of Courtney's soft voice pulled Kace out of his torturous thoughts. "Tell me exactly what you want to know."

Kace felt the moisture dampen his upper lip. "For starters," he swallowed with apparent difficulty, "you can tell me about your family."

Courtney shrugged. "There's not really much to tell. Well, my parents are both deceased—my mother died three years ago. No brothers or sisters. And my closest relatives are an aunt and two uncles in Texas, whom I rarely visit." She shifted uncomfortably. "See, I told you my life was unexciting."

His lips moved in faint smile. "Okay, now Paper-Work-Plus. I want to hear all about that."

Courtney rolled her eyes upward. "You sure are a hard taskmaster," she retorted. When he didn't respond, she plunged on with a shrug of her slim shoulders. "I graduated from Louisiana Tech with a degree in business management with a minor in computer sciences." She paused to sip her drink. "I worked for various companies until Mom died. And then I used part of my inheritance to open my own business." She smiled. "Now, my life's an open book. You know everything."

An unfathomable expression flittered across his face. "No, not everything," Kace stressed mildly. "I don't know about the men in your life—especially the one responsible for the haunted look I see lurking in the depths of your eyes."

Courtney was taken aback but refused to let him know it. "I'm sorry, I don't follow you," she said shortly. She had no intention of sharing any more of her past with him. Feigned innocence, she felt, was the best way to nip this conversation in the bud.

His eyes narrowed into a lazy measuring look. "You follow me all right," he replied smoothly, "but I won't press the issue right now."

Courtney shivered. Was that a warning? she wondered. What difference could it possibly make to him anyway? One needed to know the past only if there was to be a future. And they had no future.

"How old are you, Courtney?" Kace continued, breaking into her disquieting thoughts.

"Twenty-nine."

He smiled wryly. "Do you realize I'm nearly fifteen years older than you?"

"Yes."

"And does that bother you?"

51

"No—no, it doesn't," she admitted, circling her lips once again with the tip of her tongue. And it didn't. Not now. Not at this moment. Twenty or fifty, it mattered not. After tonight, she wouldn't be seeing him again unless it was strictly business.

"I wish you wouldn't do that."

"What?"

"Wet your lips like that."

"Oh."

Then her throat slammed shut. The husky tone of his voice and the way he was looking at her made further speech impossible. His penetrating gaze probed first her lips, then traveled downward to her heaving breasts and back up to rest on her face, her eyes.

In that one split second, everything changed. Gone was the easy talk, the laughter. A hint of something else now hung in the air between them—a sense of waiting, a kind of awareness. Each moment they spent together, she felt herself being drawn closer and closer into his net of pure sensuality.

The deep dark glow that radiated from his eyes shook her to the very core.

"Kace—"

The waiter chose that moment to appear with their food, much to Courtney's relief. The tension between them eased somewhat as he served the soup and the crabmeat special. In spite of the fact that her stomach was churning, she realized she hadn't eaten all day, and she managed to eat almost all of her dinner.

Shortly Kace pushed his plate away and beckoned for the waiter to bring them an after-dinner liqueur. Looking at his watch, he announced with a sigh, "We have only about thirty minutes to enjoy our drinks before we have to head for the stadium. The traffic will be terrible if we wait too long."

Courtney nodded. "I'm ready when you are." The air was still charged with too much emotional tension to suit her anyway.

Amusement played across his features as he seemed to be aware of her agitation. "Don't worry, Courtney, I plan to keep my word. You can relax."

Her cheeks grew warm under his steady regard.

"Go ahead, finish your drink. Our time's running out."

"And you haven't even told me *your* life history. Turnabout's fair play, you know." The words came out in a breathless rush.

"Talk about dull!" Kace chuckled softly.

"There's no way that could be true!" Courtney exclaimed.

"Well, let's see," Kace drawled. "Where should I begin the tale of my adventuresome, exciting life." His eyes twinkled.

"Come on, you're stalling, wasting precious seconds of the time we have left." She smiled readily as her good humor was somewhat restored.

"All right. You win." He grinned in return. "Let's see, I've been in the building business about fifteen years now. Before that, I was a high school football coach. I—"

"Are you joking?" Courtney interrupted with an incredulous look on her face.

"Nope. I couldn't be more serious."

Courtney cocked her head to one side. "Somehow I can't see you as a coach."

His mouth turned downward. "To be perfectly honest,

I didn't last at it long." He shrugged lightly. "Oh, I liked it well enough, the challenge was there, but the money wasn't." His features sobered. "By then I had a wife and child to support, so I went into the building business full time."

Courtney felt an unidentifiable emotion circle her heart at the mention of his wife. She was naturally curious about his marriage but couldn't quite bring herself to ask him about it. Now that he had mentioned it, however, she hoped he would say more.

"When my wife died," he went on, "I worked night and day, and before I knew it, my business had grown by leaps and bounds." He grinned ruefully. "My daughter, Susan, finally convinced me that all work and no play made daddy a dull guy. So . . ."

"So," she finished the sentence for him, "you're making up for lost time." She couldn't help but feel a twinge of disappointment at his failure to talk more about his wife and his marriage.

"Was," he declared. "Hunting season is now over."

Courtney looked puzzled. "I'm afraid I don't follow you."

"Oh, yes you do," he stated caustically. "But I'll repeat it. I said I was looking, but now I've found what I want, so hunting season is over."

Courtney felt the color tinge her cheeks. "Kace—"

"I can wait, honey, I can wait." His expression was warmly mocking.

Courtney shook her head in agitation. "You're absolutely impossible," she huffed.

His roar of laughter was infectious, and she couldn't help smiling a little. Then he changed the subject. "By the way, I plan to take you to meet my daughter and her husband first chance I get. I think you and Susan will get along just fine—just fine indeed."

Kace paid the check, and they walked briskly to the car, their bodies close, although not actually touching. After they were settled in, the silver Mercedes zoomed its way back across town. It wasn't long before they found themselves jammed into the slow-paced traffic on Poydras Street, which would eventually lead them into the stadium parking lot.

Beyond, the lights of the Superdome shone bright and clear, enhancing Courtney's sense of excitement and anticipation. She hated to admit it, but she was actually enjoying herself.

She turned toward Kace and smiled. Catching her movement, he gave her a quick wink, causing her heart to do a somersault. Sparks flared between them, and neither did anything to break the mood.

After finally being able to park the car, they made it through the jostling crowd into the massive structure. Courtney's eyes widened as she took in the capacity crowd and the pomp and ceremony taking place on the field.

"I'm glad we got here in time to see a little of the pregame show," Kace murmured close to her ear.

"So . . . so am I," Courtney stammered as his warm breath fanned across her ear, causing chill bumps up and down her spine. Damn! She needed to get a tighter rein on her emotions, she reminded herself glumly, or she was going to be in big trouble. It was frightening how attracted she was to this man. Why was she finding it so difficult to remain aloof with him as she had in the past with countless others?

Realizing they were approaching the stairway, Courtney made herself pay attention to her surroundings. She would hate to fall flat on her face right here in front of everyone.

After climbing only a short distance, Kace led her into box seats that were close to the twenty-yard line. Her dark eyes forming velvet pools, she looked up at him and laughed. "Would you believe that I don't even know who's playing?"

The musical tone of her voice and the liquid brightness of her eyes caused Kace to experience a tightening in the lower regions of his body. Whoa! Slow down! he cautioned himself. You'll have her running scared again if you don't keep your cool. But God, it was so hard when all he wanted to do was take her home and make love to her until they were both exhausted.

Courtney sensed his wandering mind and reached over and laid her hand tentatively on his arm. "Kace?"

Dark color swept up to his hairline as he looked down at the hand laying on his arm. He swallowed hard. "I'm sorry, honey," he apologized, giving her hand a quick squeeze before letting it go. "It's fifth-ranked Georgia against top-ranked Pittsburgh."

She wrinkled her nose. "Doesn't sound like it'll be much of a contest to me. Does it to you?"

"Huh," he snorted. "You just wait and see. Georgia will probably tear 'em up. This has been the season for all the number one teams to get whipped." He grinned, holding up two crossed fingers. "At least, I hope so. I've got a lot riding on the blue and gold."

Courtney grinned slyly. "Mmmmm, in that case," she quipped, "I think I'll root for Pittsburgh. It just might teach you never to bet."

Kace raised his eyebrows in mock horror. "Woman, them's fightin' words! You mean to tell me you hope that I'll lose the entire dollar I bet on this game?"

Courtney looked at him in wide-eyed confusion for several seconds before it dawned on her what he'd actually said; then they both burst out laughing.

When Courtney finally got control of herself, she breathed a sigh of relief. For a moment there, she thought she had really put her foot in her mouth. She could envision Kace having thousands of dollars riding on the outcome of this game. She knew that betting on football games was common practice in certain circles.

"You see," Kace's voice held a smile, "my son-in-law, Bob, attended the University of Pittsburgh before coming down South." His eyes sparkled. "Hence the reason for the big bet. Bob and Susan would have been here tonight, except they had a prior commitment they couldn't get out of."

"That's too bad."

"Bob thought so too. But it was a company function, and the big boss expected him to be there."

"You'll just have to give him a blow-by-blow account, then," she remarked, smiling.

"Oh, don't worry," Kace moaned. "He'll grill me for hours."

Shortly, the referee's whistle blew loud and clear, signaling the start of the game. Time passed quickly for Courtney. The game was an exciting one with each team scoring its share of touchdowns. The half-time pageantry was beautifully executed with all the bands and the spectacular display of flags. It would have been worth coming to the stadium just to see that, she thought. It was breathtaking. The game ended with the Pitt Panthers victorious over the Georgia Bulldogs. Kace took her ribbing good-naturedly.

In a way she was sorry when it ended, but Kace calmly assured her, much to her chagrin, that she would get her fill of football next year because he had season tickets to the Saints' games. Sooner or later, she fumed inwardly, she had to make him understand he couldn't control her life! Or make decisions for her!

The trek to the car didn't take long, even in the throng of people. Kace, with his long gait, took a hold of her arm and before she knew it, she was in the warm comfort of his car.

Starting the motor and quickly flipping the heat button to high, Kace maneuvered them out of the parking lot nearly as quickly as they had gotten out of the stadium.

After riding in companionable silence for a while, Courtney finally realized that they weren't headed in the direction of her home.

"Where are we going?" she asked.

"I thought we'd stop by my place for a nightcap before I take you home," he announced calmly.

Courtney's pulse leaped at the thought of being in his company a while longer. But what if . . . No, she chided herself, he promised he wouldn't crowd her or try to push her into a corner. He had given his word, and she believed him. Only she couldn't figure him out, and that concerned her. What kind of game was he really playing? His possessive remarks were anything but lighthearted. She wished she knew his real motives for pursuing her.

"Do you have any objections?"

She heard the question as if from a great distance;

shaking her head, she forced herself to concentrate on what he was saying.

"Objections?" she echoed unevenly. "No, no, I have no objections." At least not at the moment, she added silently.

It didn't take long to reach Kace's home. Like Courtney's it was in a new condominium complex, but in a more exclusive section of town. The complex was McCord designed and built, and it was awe inspiring. Kace pointed out to her that most of his complexes were patterned after this particular one.

After being escorted inside, Courtney was even more impressed. The split-level design was stunning in its elegant simplicity. Stepping into the den, she felt her feet sink into the sumptuous burnt orange carpeting on the floor. Her gaze quickly registered the soft beige velvet sofa that sat invitingly close to the corner fireplace and the circular staircase that wound to the second floor. From there one could look out over the beam-ceilinged den.

Kace crossed the room and pressed a switch upon the wall. The matching beige drapes opened with a swish to fully reveal a wall consisting entirely of glass. A sliding glass panel in the center opened onto a deck.

Kace flipped another switch, instantly dimming the indirect lighting to a warm glow. The room was further bathed in dancing shadows from the cheerfully burning logs in the fireplace. Courtney stood mesmerized by the coziness of the room and didn't hear Kace come up behind her.

"Here, let me take your coat."

His soft voice close to her ear played havoc with her

already drugged senses. But he didn't linger after removing the lightweight jacket from her shoulders. He moved to the entrance closet where he hung it on a hanger.

"Now," he said, moving toward her once again, "I want you to get comfortable on the sofa while I get us some white wine." He smiled at her tenderly. "Or would you prefer something else?"

Denying the pulsing knot that had suddenly formed in her stomach, she returned his smile with one of her own. "No," she demurred. "Whatever you're having will be fine with me."

"I'll return shortly," he told her warmly. "Don't go away." His eyes held a dark smoldering look before he turned and made his way out of the room.

She breathed shakily as she leaned her head against the inviting softness of the velvet cushions. She glanced up a short time later and saw Kace coming with a wine bucket in one hand and two glasses in the other.

"This apartment is beautiful, and it seems comfortable too," she acknowledged with a smile, as she sat up, arching her back to try and bring some energy back into her lazy muscles.

There was complete silence in the room. She heard the sharp intake of his breath as his eyes took in the burgeoning fullness of her breasts. How he ached to hold them in his hand, to bring them to pulsating hardness.

Striving to show none of his gut-felt emotions, Kace breathed deeply and smiled. "Thank you," he said, as he sat the bucket and glasses on the table in front of Courtney. "I'd be lying if I didn't say I wasn't proud of what I've accomplished."

Then in one smoothly executed movement, he sat down beside her, leaned over, and filled the glasses, handing one to her. "Here's to every moment we spend together," he said softly, raising his glass to click with hers.

Over the rim of the glass, her eyes held his for a long moment before falling before his gaze. She gave all of her attention to sipping the mellow liquid. Anything, she told herself, to keep her hands and mind busy, and off of his warm scented body so close to her own.

As if in slow motion, Kace leaned over and slowly took the glass of wine from her trembling fingers and placed it on the table.

"Courtney," he groaned huskily, "I've got to kiss you—touch you. Please—don't stop me."

4

Courtney's body began to quiver with eager anticipation but, why start something that she had no intention of finishing? she asked herself objectively. On the other hand, what was the harm in letting him kiss her—one last time?

Seeing the tug-of-war across her features, Kace moved closer to her and placed his hands on her shoulders. "You wouldn't deny a man dying of thirst, a drink of water, now would you, honey?" he asked hoarsely, urgently. His lips hovered above hers. She could feel his warm, scented breath as it gently caressed her face.

"I—"

Her hesitation proved to be her downfall. Kace took full advantage of her indecision and lay his warm lips against the parted sweetness of hers. At first it was a light experimental kiss, testing her reaction. But as she sat in stunned immobility, he increased the intensity, kissing her long and deep. It was a joyous union, each sipping on the delights of the other's mouth.

Of their own volition, Courtney's arms reached up to circle his neck, letting her fingers pilgrimage through the thickness of his soft silver mane. Her body was hot and then cold. The down on her arms stood on end at the plundering thoroughness of his mouth and tongue. But the voice in her brain whispered, Don't do this, yes, do this, do whatever you want to me, don't ever stop, please stop. . . .

"Courtney!" he whispered, sounding choked. Her quivering response served only to heighten his already enormous appetite for her.

He cupped her face in his hands and rained butterfly kisses across her eyes, her temple, and downward to her earlobe. He nibbled and licked the sensitive skin of her ear. It was as if he were an artist painting circles with his tongue.

As he continued his assault on her senses, Courtney felt their bodies slide along the back of the couch, until they rested in a half-sitting, half-lying position, in the plushness of the cushions.

"Kace!"

Her dazed gasp did nothing to deter his wandering mouth or hands. His fingers were busy unbuttoning her sweater while his mouth was on her throat, the side of her neck, and then journeying lower to the creamy expanse of the shoulder he had bared.

There he became once again the artist, using his tongue to paint circles on her shoulders and then moving lower to the fullness of her breast, now completely free of the confining undergarment. He molded each breast in his hand, where they received the loving stroke of his tongue as he painted circle after circle around her nipples.

"Please Kace—I can't stand—no don't," she pleaded thickly. She was being pulled further and further down into this vortex of sensual delights, and if she didn't call a halt soon, she told herself, it would be too late.

"Shh, honey, don't talk," he managed to rasp. His warm breath tantalized her nakedness as his mouth moved back to hover over hers. She slid down slightly, offering her mouth to his.

Yes, Kace was right, she thought. Now was not the time for talking or listening. It was the time to feel. Only feelings counted at this moment. And her body was on fire as it melted next to his. She could feel him pressing into her thigh as they lay side by side on the couch, the crackling fire the only sound in the room. She wasn't playing games with a mere boy in his adolescence but a virile and healthy man used to appeasing his appetites.

This thought served as a warning bell inside Courtney's head. "Kace—please—let me up." She tried to divert her face from his seeking, questing mouth, but without success.

Kace's mouth found her bottom lip and began gently chewing and sucking on it with his teeth. "Oh, no." Her voice sank to a low cry.

"Oh, yes, yes," he whispered as he kissed her again and again. At the same time, he closed a hand over her breast and thought that nothing he had touched had ever been softer or more beautiful. Nothing.

But soon his wandering hands weren't completely

satisfied so they began roaming from her pulsating breast to her thigh. He caressed and wooed her there until he felt compelled to search for further treasures. He slowly began to raise her skirt, his touch as light as a feather.

"Please, Courtney," he groaned, "don't make me take you home tonight. Stay with me."

"No—don't ask . . ."

"Oh, God, you don't know what you're doing to me, what you've already done to me. I've become addicted to your smell, your touch, your sweet breasts." He paused, swallowing hard. "And," he continued, his voice seductively intoxicating, "I want more—I want all of you."

The warning bells this time went off, not with just a tingle but with a roaring clang. "No!" she cried, trying almost frantically to disengage herself from his strong arms.

In a rational moment, Courtney realized that if Kace chose not to let her go there would be nothing she could do. There was no mistake about it, he was in superb physical condition, having not an ounce of excess weight anywhere on his body. She was certainly no match for him.

"Courtney, what the hell?" he muttered incoherently as he tried to pin her floundering arms against his chest.

"Let me up, I want to go home," she choked, tears edging her eyelashes.

Kace drew in a rugged breath, and then slowly folded her in the circle of his arms. "Hush, honey," he demanded softly. "Didn't I give you my word I wouldn't do anything you didn't want me to?" She shook her head up and down against his chest. "Well, all right, then, woman," he added, humor lacing his voice, "you'd best dry those tears, so I can take you home."

Sitting up fully now, Kace let her go and moved across the room to the bar to pour himself a drink. This gave Courtney time to get her clothing back in order, although with trembling fingers it was difficult. By the time Kace returned with a drink in his hand, she had herself pretty well back together—at least on the outside, she clinically observed. Inside, she was a quivering mass of contradictions: attraction, excitement on the one hand; mortification and humiliation on the other. She kept her face averted, not wanting him to see anything of her torn thoughts.

"Courtney, look at me?" he sighed at length.

She glanced up to see a liquid sweetness pouring from his eyes. She caught her breath and held it.

"Sooner or later we have to talk."

"Kace, you're wasting . . ." she began, only to be interrupted by his hand.

"No, Courtney," he stated unequivocally. "It's you who's wasting your time and thoughts if you think just because I didn't succeed in getting you in my bed tonight that I'm going to give you up."

Courtney flushed deeply.

"Well, let me assure you," he went on, "that I'm not!" He paused, lowering his voice to a soft intimate tone. "I need you, and I want you, like I need and want the air I breathe. You're mine, Courtney, make no mistake about that!"

Again his words left her speechless. At the moment, however, she was too tired, too weary, to even try and think of a suitable rejoinder to those brashly spoken words. All she seemed able to do at this point was stare at him wide-eyed and open-mouthed.

"Close your mouth, honey," he laughed softly as he made his way to the closet to get her cape. "It's time I took you home."

Moving slowly, she tried to wrap a cloak of nonchalance around her as she moved toward him, but she failed miserably. His eyes twinkled in the dancing firelight as he placed the coat around her shoulders and squeezed them.

"You're beautiful, Courtney," he whispered gently close to her ear. "All of you. And before too long, I'll know every inch of your delectable body as well as you do." As he spoke, he turned her around, his dark blue eyes staring into her uncertain ones.

"Kace, please don't say things like that to me," she said, her voice unsteady. "I know I'm—I'm confused, but I do know one thing." She compressed her lips. "I'm not about to become involved with you or any . . ."

He reached up and cut her words off with his finger across her mouth. "I know a much more effective way to shut you up," he warned thickly. "But lucky for you, I'm not up to starting something I know won't be finished tonight."

Courtney felt her face drain of every ounce of color. "Why, you, you," she spluttered, only to have Kace turn her around and march her out the door, closing it firmly behind them.

The short trip home was a silent one. Courtney's energy was so drained she couldn't have carried on a conversation even if she had wanted to. After Kace parked in front of her condominium, they walked to the front door where she fumbled around in her purse looking for the key.

With deft fingers, Kace took the purse from her hand and after one quick dip into it came up with the key. He grinned, dangling it in front of her.

In spite of herself, Courtney smiled. It was impossible, she fumed to herself, to stay irritated with him for very long. In her state of vulnerability, she couldn't combat his magnetic charm.

Taking her chin between his thumb and forefinger, Kace leaned toward her. A deep frown drew his thick eyebrows together. "I hate it like hell, but I've got to be out of town for the next two or three days." A tiny flame leapt in his eyes as his thumb caressed her chin. "But the minute I get back, our date still stands to visit my daughter."

Courtney lowered her eyelids and then raised them defensively. His thumb ceased its exploration but remained stationary.

"Kace, I wish you wouldn't plan . . ." she began, haltingly.

"Courtney, I refuse to argue with you anymore tonight." A faint smile lifted the corners of his lips. "Anyway," he challenged warmly, "haven't you learned by now you're wasting precious energy arguing with me?" His hand moved up to caress her cheek gently.

The smoothing touch of his fingers on her face had the desired effect. They stilled her mouth—made it almost impossible for her to speak much less argue with him. She was too tired, anyway. She was numb with fatigue and overcharged emotions.

His eyes moved over her face taking in the unflawed

paleness of her skin enhanced by the smudged darkness underneath her eyes.

"You're dead on your feet," he murmured with a sigh. "I need to go home and let you get ready for bed."

"I am tired," she agreed huskily. She glanced up at him, her eyes pools of green velvet.

There was a teasing smile in his eyes, and Courtney wondered what he was thinking.

"Do I need to come in and help you put on your 'jammies?"

"I don't wear—uh—'jammies."

"You wear a nightgown, then?"

"No, I don't wear a nightgown."

Silence.

"Well, then, what do you wear?"

"Nothing."

Kace sucked in his breath, then expelled it slowly. "I'll pay you back for that, Courtney Roberts," he rasped. "You can mark it down!"

"Goodnight, Kace," she said softly, closing the door on his torture-ridden expression.

What had awakened her? What time was it? Rolling over, Courtney lifted heavy laden eyelids and looked at the lighted digital clock next to her bed; it registered twelve o'clock. Finally it penetrated her befuddled brain that it was the telephone's shrill ring that was making the obtrusive noise. Who could be calling her at this ungodly hour of the morning? she wondered.

Groggily she reached for the phone. Before she could say anything a male voice said, "Courtney, I'm sorry to wake you but I just got in and I . . ."

"Kace?" she cut in, her voice hesitant, "Is something wrong?" He sounded tired. Depressed? She felt a momentary pang of concern hit her.

"No, honey," he sighed wearily, "nothing's wrong." He paused briefly. "For one thing, I just wanted to hear your voice. And for another, I wanted to let you know I'll pick you up at eight o'clock. Pack a bag, because in all likelihood we'll probably spend the night with Susan and Bob."

Now Courtney was wide awake, her concern swiftly disappearing to be replaced by frustration. "Kace! No! I can't, what I mean is, I won't—"

"Go back to sleep, Courtney," he said, as if she hadn't spoken. "I'll see you in the morning."

The light click on the other end of the line told Courtney that she was holding a dead instrument. After reaching over and placing the phone back in its cradle, she flopped back against the pillows.

Undoubtedly, Kace McCord was the most obstinate, hard-headed man she had ever known! He never listened to a word she said. She might as well be talking to the wind as to talk to him, she thought angrily. She would just have to make him understand when he came to the door that she had no intention of going with him. This time, she promised herself, she would remain firm, no matter how much she had missed him and longed to see him.

During his absence, she had worked hard, but no amount of work had been able to keep her thoughts from lingering on what had taken place between them the night of the ballgame. Her stomach still churned every time she thought about the way his mouth and tongue had ravaged her body. Each day she had carried around with her an unfulfilled ache which she found disconcerting. She'd silently battled against those memories, but they adhered to her mind like glue.

Now the disruptive phone call made it more impossible than ever to sleep. The rest of the night was a total loss. She tossed and turned until six o'clock. Deciding she was wasting good time and energy, she crawled out of the bed.

She padded to the window and raised the wooden shades to a beautiful morning. It was rare in New Orleans to have a Saturday in January that was clear and crisp. She stretched her tired muscles trying to muster up the courage to shower, dress, and prepare for the battle ahead with Kace. The last being no small feat, she thought humorlessly.

In spite of what she had facing her, Courtney found herself actually enjoying getting ready for his arrival. She took a long leisurely shower, washing her thick hair until it was squeaky clean. She repainted her fingernails and toenails with a luscious burgundy frost which matched her lipgloss.

After drying her hair and curling the blunt ends with a curling iron, she sat down to apply her makeup. She applied it sparsely as her magnolia-perfect skin needed little else to enhance its beauty.

Since she had no intention of going with Kace, she decided to dress casually. She planned to spend part of the day washing clothes, shopping the January clearance sales, and exercising at the spa. So she donned a pair of corduroys and a pullover velour sweater, minus a bra since she would have to change later into her leotard.

At exactly eight o'clock, the doorbell chimed. Nervously raking a hand through her hair, Courtney opened the door. Her heart skidded to a stop at the sight of Kace. He too was dressed in jeans and a blue sweater, which enhanced the beauty of his eyes.

A light sprang into his face as his searching gaze met hers. They looked into each other's eyes, and Courtney found herself wanting to touch him—touch his face, his eyes, his lips. She felt herself drifting toward him.

Kace stepped into the room and kicked the door shut behind him. It wasn't clear who made the first move. They found themselves wrapped in each other's arms.

No words passed between them; none were necessary.

Kace was trying to exhibit rigid control as he folded her closer to him, seeking her mouth. The fleeting taste of her body the other night had only made him want her all the more. The last few days he had felt as if he were on the verge of starvation.

Courtney instantly knew the insistence of his tongue; she opened herself to him, letting him pillage and plunder at will. Shaken and breathing in gasps, she tore her mouth away, managing to end the devastating attack on her senses.

"Good morning," he whispered, transferring his lips to the side of her neck where he savored the delicious smell of her.

"Good morning to you too," she echoed none too steadily. She then tried to pull away from him.

"Courtney?"

She glanced up wide-eyed, only to meet his lips as they reached for hers again, hungrily. Finally he released her, albeit reluctantly, and pushed her firmly away from him.

"Go get your bag and let's get out of here," he ordered

huskily. A muscle flared in his jaw showing his still tight control.

Courtney shook her head. "I'm—I'm not going."

His nostrils flared. "Go get your bag, Courtney," he repeated. The timbre of his voice was now dangerously low.

Courtney willed herself not to move. "No," she said firmly.

"Damn it, woman," he bellowed. "I've about had it with your stubbornness. Now go get your bag."

Courtney bit her lower lip to keep from trembling. She felt hot tears well up in her eyes.

Seeing the stricken look on her face, Kace's features softened considerably. He rubbed the back of his neck before saying carefully, "Forget the bag for now. Let's just go and get something to eat." He paused, lines deepening around his mouth. "And talk. Please."

She could only nod, her throat suddenly constricted. Damn him! she thought. Why couldn't he ever take no for an answer? And why couldn't she ever mean what she said and stick to it? She felt frustrated and angry at herself for her weakness toward him. Hot tears pricked her eyelids.

An uneasy silence accompanied them on the way to the coffee shop. By the time Kace had parked the car, Courtney's nerves felt raw and exposed.

After being seated and ordering their breakfast, Kace was the first to break the silence. But it wasn't what Courtney wanted to hear. "Please tell me," he asked tautly, "what happened to make you so distrustful of me," he spread his hands, "and of men in general."

Hot anger shot through her at his persistence.

He read her mind like a book. And before she could say a word, he went on. "I know what you're thinking," he sighed. "I know you're madder than hell at me right now for asking about your past again, but I've got to know!" She could hear the underlying core of steel in his voice. "If nothing else, for my own sanity—my own peace of mind."

The fight went out of Courtney. She stared down at her hands, which were clenched in her lap. Why not tell him, she thought dejectedly. Why not get it over with once and for all? What had happened to her had happened to a lot of other women. And hadn't she recognized a long time ago that the majority of her remorse was more a case of wounded pride than broken heart? But the thought of talking about it aloud—airing her dirty laundry, so to speak—was another matter altogether.

"What happened?" he pressed softly.

Courtney felt her palms grow damp. She swallowed hard. "Two days before our big church wedding, my senior year in college, I walked into my fiancé's apartment and caught him in bed with my roommate." A tremor shook her voice. "I had naively believed that I was the only one in Hal's life." Bitterness was now the predominant emotion in her voice.

Kace started to interrupt.

Courtney held up her hand. "Please," she demanded hoarsely, "let me finish. Remember you asked." She paused to take a sip of her coffee. Her lips were uncomfortably dry. "So," she continued, "to make a long story short, I walked out of his apartment and out of his life. But that wasn't all." She paused briefly. "The next day I received a note saying that he and Marilyn had eloped and were leaving the country. Of course, I was left with the gifts, the . . ." Her voice trailed off to nothing.

The increasing tension began to draw stares from the surrounding tables. Courtney was positive everyone in the restaurant could hear her pounding heart. But for some unknown reason, Courtney found she actually felt better. It was as if, by telling him, she had opened a wound that had been festering for years. Now maybe it would slowly but surely relieve her of all the poison she had kept inside for so long.

When they were no longer the center of attention, Kace looked at her, his eyes filled with deep longing and tenderness. "You do know you never have to fear anything like that ever happening with me, don't you?" he asked huskily. His hand reached across the table and clasped her slender fingers tightly within his. "You can trust your love in my hands, my darling. I'll never misuse it or abuse it. You believe me, don't you?"

Courtney swallowed the lump in her throat. "It's going to take time, I still—"

His gaze softened. "I know. You don't have to say any more. We'll take it one day at a time." He grinned. "How about starting now? By going to my daughter's? Are you game—clothes or no clothes?"

Her heart turned over at the eagerness in his voice. And when it came down to it, she didn't want to refuse him. She wanted to be with him. "All right. You win." She smiled, some of the tension leaving her face. "But I'm chalking up my temporary insanity to the beautiful sunshiny day! Do you understand what I'm saying, Kace McCord?"

His roar of laughter turned many a head in their direction as they left the restaurant—breakfast forgotten.

The hundred and twenty-four–mile trip to Lafayette, where his daughter and son-in-law lived, proved to be an enjoyable one for Courtney. Very little conversation passed between them after the first few miles, so Courtney made use of the time by trying to relax. Her lack of sleep the night before and her emotional morning had finally caught up with her. As the silver Mercedes ate up the miles, Courtney felt her eyelids become heavier and heavier until she finally closed them to the sound of Kace's soft chuckle.

The only stop they made was to zip through a fast food drive-in window for an order of tacos and Cokes. Even though it was a messy treat, they continued to eat them as they traveled. Shortly the car was filled with laughter as the sauce decorated both their faces and hands. Instead of stopping at a gas station to clean up, they used a small bottle of lotion and tissue Courtney kept in her purse to make the visible enjoyment of their lunch disappear.

It was times like this that Courtney realized her vulnerability where Kace was concerned. And it frightened her still, the power he had over her physical responses. Now, as she sat next to him, she ached to reach over and touch him. Out of the corner of her eye, she could see his clearly defined profile—the fine chiseled nose down to the jutting chin. And his legs, which were molded by his jeans like a second skin, drew her unwilling attention to his masculinity.

When they reached the outskirts of Lafayette, however, a sense of uneasiness crept over her as it dawned on her that she was soon to meet Kace's daughter, Susan.

She couldn't help but wonder what reactions Susan would have about her father seeing someone only a few years older than herself? And what did she, Courtney, think? Did it bother her? In all honesty, she had to admit that it made the situation a little less than ideal.

Kace had led her to believe that Susan would like her, that they would get along just fine. But she wasn't so sure. What if Susan was the possessive type of daughter who didn't want to share her father with another woman? Especially one so close to her own age?

But why should she care what Kace's family thought about her? Her age? Their relationship? She knew that she and Kace had no future, so why did these questions rattle around in her head and trouble her so?

"Hey, I'm jealous," Kace remarked softly, bringing her disturbed thoughts sharply back into focus.

Her eyebrows drew together in a puzzled frown as she turned in the seat to face him. "What on earth made you say a thing like that?" she asked.

Kace's mouth was oddly twisted. "Your mind was a million miles away from me just now, wasn't it?"

Courtney's cheeks became tinged with pink. She had no intention of letting him know her thoughts. They were definitely not for sharing.

She shifted restlessly. "Well, what difference does it make one way or the other?"

"You just don't understand yet, do you?"

She shook her head. "No—no, I guess I don't," she stated blankly.

"Well, I'm jealous of anything you say, do, or think which takes you away from me," Kace said, his eyes lowering to the rounded swell of her breasts.

Courtney felt again that curling sensation in the pit of her stomach. She felt too the pouting hardness of her nipples as they pushed against her sweater. For a few paralyzing moments the tension was so thick it was almost overpowering.

Kace laughed, expelling it somewhat, as he turned and gave driving his full attention once again. "If I don't quit getting sidetracked," he averred unsteadily, "you may end up meeting Susan and Bob from a hospital bed."

"Oh, I'm not worried. I trust you completely," she replied, as she concentrated on settling her erratic breathing.

"I wish you meant that," Kace countered quietly.

They both knew he wasn't referring to his driving skills, but Courtney refused to be drawn into another confrontation, as she chose to let it slide.

"Are we nearly there? Are you sure they're expecting me to be with you?" Courtney knew she was rattling in order to cover up her agitation. But once again she found herself not in control of a situation, and it irritated her.

"Yes," he replied, after maneuvering the car successfully around a road construction crew.

"Yes to what?" She blinked, trying to gather her scattered thoughts.

"Yes to are we nearly there. And yes to are they expecting you." His eyes gleamed in devilish amusement.

"Are you sure?" she insisted, ignoring his gleaming eyes.

"Yes," he sighed. "I'm sure. Relax. Susan asked me to bring you. Okay?" His eyes searched her face briefly.

Courtney nibbled at her lower lip. "Okay," she acquiesced, with a shrug of her slender shoulders. "If you say so."

A short time later, Kace pulled up in front of what looked to be a newly constructed house. It was in an exclusive suburb of Lafayette. The city proper had grown so rapidly with the oil craze that had attacked it that the majority of the population had moved to the outer areas.

Watching him turn off the ignition, Courtney remarked, "I assume your son-in-law works for one of the big oil companies." Her eyes perused the opulent ranch-style home with its perfectly manicured lawn.

"That's right," Kace drawled levelly. "He's working himself up into a top-notch executive position with Sun Oil." There was a hint of mockery in his eyes. "If you're thinking I had any influence in helping him climb the ladder of corporate success, you couldn't be more wrong. He's done it all on his own."

"Kace, I didn't mean . . ."

He leaned over and planted a quick kiss on her lips. "I know you didn't. I just wanted to set the record straight, that's all."

Following those words, Kace hastened out of the car and came around to open her door. As he reached for her hand, the front door was opened with an excited cry, and out came a beautiful young woman followed by a man.

Courtney's breath caught in her throat. It was obvious, very obvious indeed that Susan McCord Davis was expecting a baby!

5

─∞∞∞∞∞∞∞∞─

"Why didn't you tell me?" Courtney demanded in a hissing whisper.

Impatience hardened Kace's irises as he leaned closer to her. "What the hell?" he began roughly, only to have his words brought to an abrupt halt by the approach of his daughter and son-in-law behind him. He turned to face them.

"Oh, Daddy," exclaimed a radiant Susan as she flung herself into Kace's outstretched arms. He smiled tenderly into his daughter's upturned face, none of the agitation of a split second ago showing on his own.

Courtney, as she leaned heavily against the car, felt very much an outsider. There was loving affection on both sides as Kace was given a hearty handshake and a slap on the back by his son-in-law. And Susan was still clinging to his arm like a vine. Their immersement in each other gave Courtney time to reorient her scattered emotions from the shock of discovering Susan was pregnant. Why this should have upset her so, she didn't know, but it did. She plastered a smile across her face as her host and hostess turned their attention toward her.

"Hello, Courtney," Susan smiled shyly. "I'm Susan, and this is my husband Bob. We're so glad you could come."

"Thank you for inviting me," Courtney replied softly, studying the younger woman as she placed her hand momentarily in Susan's outstretched one. The resemblance to Kace was uncanny. Susan had the same perfectly chiseled features as her father, and on her they were beautiful. Her hair was dark brown and framed her face in glowing brightness. She was tall and willowy; her pregnancy enhanced her good looks rather than distracted from them. When she smiled, she became the almost exact replica of Kace, causing Courtney's heart to turn over.

Standing next to Susan, her husband Bob looked to be exactly her height. A wiry mop of russet curls topped his head, and there was a splattering of freckles across the bridge of his nose. However his twinkling brown eyes and warm handshake made Courtney like him on sight.

"Well," Bob teased playfully, "I see this time Kace has fetched himself a real beauty."

Before Courtney could reply to his teasing compliment, Susan nudged her husband in the ribs. "Watch it, Bob. Courtney might not take too kindly to your brand of teasing."

"Oh," Kace interposed softly, "I think she can handle it." He smiled, but the smile never quite reached his eyes. Courtney knew he was still angry with her for her statement of a few moments ago. And just as soon as the opportunity presented itself, she felt sure he would demand an explanation. How would she answer him? she wondered.

"Dad, you two are planning on spending the night, aren't you?" Susan asked as they walked up the sidewalk toward the house.

"Oh, Susan, no, I don't think . . ." Courtney answered hurriedly, even though she knew Susan hadn't actually spoken to her.

"Yes," cut in Kace, a muscle working in his jaw. "We certainly do intend to spend the night. Wouldn't miss it for the world." The look he threw Courtney dared her to contradict him.

Courtney forced her lips to smile as she noticed the rather anxious expression Susan wore. "It's—it's fine with me, too, if you're sure it won't be too much trouble?"

Susan laughed as she patted her protruding stomach. "You can't tell it by looking, but I actually have nearly four months to go before the baby's due." She sighed, ruefully. "The doctor says I'm either going to have twins or a big baby."

Kace rolled his eyes upward. "Let's pray it'll be twins." He grinned mischievously.

Susan and Bob both let out a yelp that could be heard all over the neighborhood. "Kace McCord!" Bob grated, "if it is twins, in honor of your wish, we'll give you one to take care of." He tried to keep a straight face, but his eyes were dancing with laughter.

"Huh," Kace snorted, "if you think I wouldn't take one you're wrong. I'd welcome the challenge."

"All right, you two," Susan implored. "Quit your

arguing. There's going to be only *one* baby, and I'll keep it!"

There was good-humored laughter all around as they made their way into the warm comfort of the house.

Courtney looked around as she was ushered into the den by Bob and told to have a seat. The huge room with a high arched ceiling and two skylights dominated the entire left side of the house. To the right of the entrance hall, Courtney had noticed a formal dining room, and beyond she caught a glimpse of the kitchen. The bedrooms, she assumed, were across the back of the house.

Although large, the den projected an air of hominess which Courtney identified with immediately. There was a crackling fire in the fireplace, and the odor of burning hickory filled the room with a pleasant scent. It was tastefully decorated with wall hangings, plants, and brightly cushioned pine furniture.

"Do you like it, Courtney?" Susan smiled proudly. "Dad and Bob built it."

"It's beautiful, but more important, it's comfortable," she complimented warmly.

"That's what I like about it too," Susan declared enthusiastically. "Now," she continued breathing deeply, "I know you must be thirsty and probably hungry as well. So, Dad, why don't you show Courtney the guest room and bath while Bob helps me rustle up a quick snack." She smiled. "It won't be much, though, because Bob has a brisket on the grill for dinner tonight."

Courtney felt her stomach plummet to her toes at this sudden change of events. The last thing she wanted was to be alone with Kace. He was too quiet, too preoccupied to suit her. She knew he was just lying in wait to confront her like a cat stalking a canary.

Sensing Courtney's hesitation, Kace strode over and grasped her hand in what looked to be a loving manner, but she knew better. She could feel the steel in his grip as he pulled her up beside him and then gently prodded her in the direction of the bedrooms.

Unaware of the tension in the room, Susan and Bob took themselves off to the kitchen with excited chatter bouncing back and forth between them.

The moment they were alone, Kace opened the first door he came to and waited with hooded eyes for her to enter. He then closed the door behind him with a soft slam. He rested his muscular frame against it and appraised Courtney's slender figure with eyes the color of blue marble. "Now," he ordered grimly, "let's have it."

Courtney wrapped her arms around her upper body as if to protect herself. "Kace," she began, only to pause and wet her lips nervously, "you're making a mountain out of a mole hill. I didn't really say anything—" she broke off lamely.

"I agree. It wasn't so much what you said, but the way you said it." His voice had an ominous ring to it.

She lowered her head. "All right, so I apologize. Does that make you happy?"

"Courtney!"

She jerked her head upward in time to see Kace's nostrils flare and him jam his hands down into the pocket of his jeans. A silent alarm sent her pulse racing. She saw right then and there, he was angry. She had made what he took to be a demeaning remark against not only him but his daughter as well. He had no intention, she told herself, of settling for anything less than the truth from her. She was seeing for the first time a side of Kace that she didn't know existed. Gone were the warm smile, the tender teasing, and the loving words.

"Courtney—I'm waiting," he warned levelly, breaking into her silent musings. "Even if it takes all day." His lips were compressed impatiently, bracketing his mouth with harsh lines.

"I was just shocked to see that Susan was pregnant, that's all," she blurted out at him, stung by his sudden hostility and overreaction to her carelessly spoken words.

"And why should that bother you?"

"Because, because, she's—" She broke off with evident distress.

"—because she's pregnant, and that means I'm going to be a grandfather. And I take it that bothers you." His voice had dropped to such a low pitch, until Courtney wasn't sure if it was a trace of hurt she detected there? Or scorn? Or a little of both?

Her tongue clung to the dry roof of her mouth. "Well, it does—it did. But," she was quick to add, "it doesn't anymore."

"And what, if I may ask, made you change your mind all of a sudden?" he inquired. This time there was no mistaking the tone of his voice. Sarcasm literally dripped from it.

Courtney felt her face suffuse with color. Damn him! For backing her into a corner—for making her feel guilty and totally in the wrong. How dare he! She didn't like this caged-in feeling, and for a moment she wanted to lash out at him. However, cold logic came to her rescue. She knew it wasn't so much what she had said about Susan but what her statement had implied to Kace. He felt it would make a difference in her feeling toward him, she was sure of it. That maybe *now* she would think he was indeed too old for her—since he was soon to be a grandfather.

Did she care what Kace thought? Yes, she did, she told herself quickly. And there was no use denying it. She drew her eyebrows together in a troubled frown as the silence deepened.

"Well, I'm waiting," he remarked softly, disturbing her anxious introspection.

When she looked up at him, he seemed more relaxed. His eyes, however, were still intently regarding her. He had straightened his tall lithe body and was no longer using the door for a support. His hands were positioned in the low waistband of his jeans. With the v-neck of his sweater exposing the brown column of his throat and his smooth silver hair brushing his neckband at his nape, he emanated such blatant sexual attraction it made her knees grow weak with longing.

Oh, no! she severely berated herself. Now was certainly not the time to think of how his hands and mouth could bring her body to such a feverish pitch. Right now, she needed to concentrate on smoothing the troubled waters.

She hastily averted her head to keep him from seeing her raw emotions so exposed. Apparently he had read her like a book once again, because Kace crossed the floor in one gigantic stride and with a gentle finger to her chin turned her around to face him.

The tormented look on his face as he gazed down at her caused sudden tears to edge Courtney's lashes.

"I—I'm sorry," she whispered, haltingly. "I—I didn't mean—"

Kace shook his head. "No, please don't say any more. I'm the one who should apologize for getting so bent out of shape over nothing." He sucked in his breath and then expelled it slowly. "But since I haven't quite made a believer out of you as to the longevity of our relationship, I had visions of you . . ." He broke off, a semblance of a grin working at the corners of his mouth. "Anyway," he went on with a sigh. "I could just see myself having to bring you back into the fold by the hair of your chinny, chin, chin." He grinned openly.

"Kace . . ."

He caressed her cheek gently with the back of his knuckles. "Is that all you know how to say, honey, is my name?"

The warmth radiating from his eyes melted any resistance she had left. He had extended an olive branch, and the least she could do was meet him halfway.

Courtney felt the tears that clung to her lashes now slowly trickle down her face. Why she was crying, she didn't know. Kace groaned and drew her close to his body. He began to rain kisses as soft and fluttering as a hummingbird's touch on the side of her neck, moving upward to her cheek, and from there nibbled a sensuous trail across to her mouth.

The familiar ache began deep inside her as she circled his waist with her arms, molding her body to the hard contour of his. "Oh, Kace, please, kiss me."

He needed no further encouragement. His mouth bore down into the softness of hers, causing her head to swim as if she'd gulped a glassful of heady wine. She heard herself groan as his tongue began a search of the inside of her mouth. Courtney felt herself being swept away to another time, another place.

The gentle tap on the door failed to penetrate either one of their befuddled senses, until the tap became a rather pronounced knock. "Dad, are you and Courtney in there?" Susan asked, her voice both timid and hesitant.

Courtney was the first to break away. She wedged her arms between them and gave Kace a firm push. He reluctantly dropped his arms and stepped backward. His eyes, were glazed as he strove to conquer his erratic breathing.

"Yes, we're in here, kitten," he finally acknowledged, his eyes now clear and centered on Courtney's face. "We're just having a little friendly discussion, that's all. We'll be out shortly."

"Uh, that's fine," Susan replied hurriedly. "We'll wait for you in the den," she added. Her footsteps could be heard as she scurried down the hall.

A small smile broke across Kace's face as he commented lightly, "I guess I can safely assume that for the time being at least, we've called a truce."

Courtney felt the blood surge to her face. She was embarrassed that Susan had caught her and Kace closeted in the room together like two teenagers. And she was equally embarrassed at how brazenly she had demanded Kace kiss her. All of a sudden, it seemed that this man with his endearing grin, his silver hair, and those twinkling blue eyes was becoming much too dear, much too familiar, and much too important to suit her.

She would never have believed in a million years that this man or any other man could cast such a spell upon her. She must come to her senses and fight it, she told herself. There was absolutely no time for a man in her life, no matter how physically drawn she was to him! But to argue with Kace here, this weekend, would be fruitless.

mind?" She paused and flashed Susan a sweet smile. "It must have been the delicious dinner."

Susan grinned in return. "We both know that's not true. But I'll accept the compliment, anyway."

"Now listen here, wife," Bob exclaimed. "I'm the one who did the majority of the cooking." He grinned. "Courtney, you're paying homage to the wrong chef."

As Courtney was unsuccessful in warding off another yawn, Kace called a halt to the interchange of camaraderie by placing his hand under Courtney's elbow and helping her up from the couch. He steered her in the direction of the guest room.

As they reached the door, Courtney turned and called to Bob and Susan, "Goodnight. And thank you both for a lovely evening. I'm sorry again that I'm such a party pooper," she added in a low voice.

"You're no party pooper," Susan declared instantly. "I'm going to bed too. Oh, before I forget, Courtney, do you need to borrow a gown or pajamas to sleep in? I noticed that neither you nor Dad brought a bag of any kind."

For a split second there was silence in the room. But Kace's amused chuckle served to jolt her into action. Courtney felt her face burn as she stammered, "I—er—I"

"Don't worry about it, kitten," Kace interrupted with laughter glimmering in his eyes, his voice. "Courtney doesn't—"

A swift and hard jab to Kace's ribcage forestalled any further comment from him. Courtney forced herself not to look at him or she believed she would have been hard pressed not to slap that amusing grin off his face.

Courtney breathed deeply. "Thank you, Susan. I'd love to borrow a gown as well as an extra toothbrush if you have them available."

Momentarily, Susan and Bob both had worn a puzzled expression on their faces; however, it disappeared with Courtney's statement.

"I have both," Susan assured quickly. "I'll bring them to your room."

The minute Courtney found herself alone with Kace, she turned on him like a spitting rattlesnake. "What do you mean," she demanded through clenched teeth, "intimating in front of Susan and Bob that I—I sleep in the nude."

Kace's eyes narrowed. "Well, don't you?"

"Well—yes," Courtney retorted, "but I wouldn't want them . . ."

Kace threw back his head and laughed. "Oh, honey, you're nothing short of a little hypocrite. Did you know that?" He paused to tap her playfully on the nose. "But I'll overlook your little idiosyncrasies if you'll come down off your high horse."

Courtney's chin jutted. "If you don't stop treating me like a child, I—I—"

Kace expelled his breath on an impatient sigh. "Treating you like a child never enters my mind when I'm around you. Quite the contrary, I'd say." His eyes darkened. "While we're on the subject of maturity, how much longer are you going to make me wait, before you admit you belong to me? One taste of your delightful body was not nearly enough," he declared huskily. "You deserve to be loved slowly and carefully—"

"No! Kace," she articulated with difficulty.

"Yes, Courtney," he countered as his eyes held hers.

Words failed her as did her breath as his bold roaming hands sufficiently robbed her of both. They journeyed slowly from her shoulders down the partial length of her arms, only to slip to her waist. Before she could stop him, his hands with their touch of velvet had slipped under her sweater and began massaging first her lower back and then around to her midriff.

Courtney was breathing now shallowly and unsteadily.

"No bra," Kace groaned, one hand cupping the fullness of one breast.

"Don't—not here. I can't—" Courtney was finding it hard to speak while his hands stroked her. She continued to struggle, which only added to Kace's frustration.

With a muffled expletive, Kace brought his ministrations to a halt. He pushed her away from him quite forcefully. "I know this isn't the time or the place to make love to you," he said with ragged breath. "But I can't give you too much more time, even though I promised." His eyes burned down into hers. "You want me and need me as much as I want and need you. And don't bother denying it!"

With those timely words he made a swift exit from the room. Courtney caught a sob in her throat as she slowly but methodically readied herself for bed. She barely smiled her thanks at Susan when she delivered the gown and toothbrush.

Sleep proved to be elusive. She rolled and tumbled until her thoughts were a jumbled-up mess. She knew beyond a shadow of a doubt that Kace had reached his limit with flirting, kissing, and touching. If she continued to see him, he had made his intentions clear. He would make love to her—he had said that.

And what about her? What were her true feelings? How did she really feel about it? In all honesty, could she deny that she wanted him to make love to her?

Fast on the heels of that question came another. What did Kace have that caused her to forget so easily the trauma she went through with Hal? Granted, he was the most exciting man she had ever known. He was nice. He was kind. He had more than his share of charm. And he stirred emotions in her body that she hadn't known existed. She was addicted to the sensations his hungry mouth and hands could arouse in her.

If she did allow Kace to make love to her, wouldn't she be leaving herself open to more hurt and disillusionment by letting him get close to her? Was she merely a challenge to him? Once he wore down her defenses, would he leave her high and dry? After all, he had never said he loved her—only that he wanted her. A relationship based solely on physical attraction rarely ever lasted. It soon disappeared like loose ashes in a windstorm.

How, then, could she overcome her powerful physical need for this man when she really didn't want to? For this was one time when her need was threatening to overrule her good judgment.

These thoughts and more kept stampeding through her mind until exhaustion finally overtook her. She finally fell into a troubled sleep.

The next morning as Kace drove the winding highway toward home, he talked about an overseas contract for more condominiums and office buildings that he was negotiating. If the deal went through, he told her, it would take him to China for at least three weeks to a month. He went on to tell her it would be another several days, however, before he would know his plans. A strange feeling settled over her at the possibility of his being away for that long a time. She refused to analyze that feeling any further.

Courtney was thankful as the miles clipped by that the unsettling events of last night were not mentioned. She didn't think she could bear another confrontation with Kace. After a delicious breakfast with Susan and Bob, Kace had been eager to make his departure, as was she. She was dreadfully tired after not having slept well for two nights straight. If Kace noticed the circles under her eyes, he failed to comment on it, much to her relief. Her emotions were already as tight as a violin string—ready to snap at a moment's notice.

The trip back to New Orleans and home was a pleasant one. Before she was aware of it, Kace was slowing the Mercedes and bringing it to a stop in front of her condominium.

He swung around to face her, his mouth turned downward. "I hate it like hell, but I'm going to be involved the next few days with that overseas project." He sighed. "So I doubt I'll get to see you much, if any. But this weekend, I want us to take my yacht out into the bay and do some saltwater fishing. How does that sound to you?"

A shiver of excited anticipation slid down Courtney's spine. "That—that sounds fine," she ventured tentatively. "I've never been on a yacht or saltwater fishing either for that matter."

A grin slashed across his features as his eyes moved

over her face, lingering on her mouth, then coming back to rest on her eyes. "That makes it even better," he murmured. He paused as his thumb stroked the dark smudges underneath her eyes. "So there won't be any misunderstanding later, we will be spending the night on board the yacht."

6

~~~~~~~~~~~~~~~~~

Courtney felt excitement grip her as she got her first glimpse of Kace's yacht, *The Majestic,* moored in its slip on Lake Pontchartrain.

Kace brought the Mercedes to an abrupt stop at the crowded dock area after pointing out his prized possession to her. He smiled as he turned off the ignition. "Wait here a minute, I'll be right back. I have to pick up some bait and notify the office of our destination."

"All right," she agreed, flexing her weary shoulder muscles against the back of the seat.

The moment she was alone, Courtney surveyed her surroundings. There was a lot of vigorous activity taking place around the marina. Others, like themselves, were obviously making plans to take advantage of this absolutely gorgeous day in late January either to fish or simply enjoy another recreational sport. The temperature was now in the lower sixties with the high predicted to be in the low to middle seventies. Perfect fishing weather, Kace had advised her with a grin.

Although she had been to Lake Pontchartrain and the amusement park many times in the past, none of those excursions had carried the emotional impact of this particular trip. The past few days had been traumatic ones for her. Since their parting at her door last Sunday evening, she had spent grueling hours at the office. As a result, she was exhausted in both mind and body. For a while, she and Amy had had no large contracts other than Kace's. Then, all of a sudden, Paper-Work-Plus had been hired to do multiple mailings for two real estate companies and a new bank. She and Amy were overjoyed at obtaining the additional contracts, but the added pressure had taken its toll on both of them, especially Courtney.

She had fought long and hard to keep thoughts of Kace at bay, but it hadn't worked. No amount of paperwork could erase him from her mind. She had vacillated between excitement and apprehension concerning the overnight fishing trip. She had asked herself the same question over and over. Would she be taking a disastrous wrong step by keeping the date with him?

She was an intelligent and mature woman, and she knew that Kace intended to try and make love to her. How would she react? Would she, once and for all, give in to her mounting desire for him and let him have what they both seemed to want? And, if she did, could she handle the repercussions from such an action? She knew that *if* she gave herself to him she would eventually have to make a decision about a commitment to Kace. Was she willing to pay the price for a moment's sexual gratification? Or was the price too high?

Afraid, unwilling, and too tired to search for the answers to those questions, she had thrust them aside and plunged that much deeper into her work.

When Kace had called for her this morning, she had only moments before slipped into her jeans and pulled a sweater over her head. It had been after eight when she had crawled out of the bed. A quick shower and a hearty breakfast had helped to revive her somewhat. But nothing could control the tremors that swept through her body, leaving her already tired limbs even weaker, when she thought about spending the night alone with Kace. As yet, the questions that had plagued her all week still hadn't been answered. But she had reached one conclusion and that was her desire to see Kace again and feel his lips against hers.

Although his greeting had been quite casual, only a quick kiss on the lips, she sensed that underneath his calm facade were explosive thoughts that would probably shock her if she knew them. He was definitely holding himself in check.

Now, as she watched him make his way out of the marina office, his long strides bringing him toward the car, she felt a hot liquid flame shoot through her body. He was dressed in jeans, rather worn and faded in places, but comfortable looking. A sweatshirt and tennis shoes completed his outfit. They too had seen better days. He appeared relaxed and happy and radiated a sensual power that drew her to him like a magnet.

She swallowed hard before flashing him a rather weak smile as he opened the car door on her side.

"Have you got your sea legs under you?" he inquired, giving her a lopsided grin.

She smiled. "I'm not sure. But I guess I'm about to find

out, aren't I?" She couldn't quite bring herself to meet his warm gaze as she answered his question.

"You betcha. And for two whole days, too. Doesn't the idea of being away from people and the telephone appeal to you?" Kace asked, his voice low and disturbing.

Courtney felt her response to his leading question stir in the base of her stomach.

In a shaky breath she replied, "As a matter of fact, it does."

Kace laughed. "Then what are we waiting for? Let's go aboard!"

After giving her arm a playful tug as he helped her out of the car, Kace reached in the glove compartment and pushed the button to release the trunk. He lifted the sack of groceries out of it, along with an ice chest, and nodded in the direction of the yacht.

Up close, the yacht was even more dazzling than Courtney had ever imagined. It was without dispute a magnificent craft. The steel and mahogany combined gave its sleek lines a lavish look.

"So this is your pride and joy," Courtney observed, her voice filled with awe.

"One of my pride and joys," he responded softly, his melting glance traveling over the soft contours of her face. His look was an almost tangible caress as it lingered there.

Courtney was momentarily hypnotized by his intent gaze. Then he looked abruptly away, breaking the spell as a crowd of loud teenagers shuffled past them.

Turning back to her, he urged gruffly, "Come on, let's go." He grinned. "These groceries are about to break my arm."

Kace dropped the chest on the deck and went directly to the galley to put the sack of food away, leaving Courtney to look at will. She noted the upper deck was furnished with brightly cushioned chairs and tables, while the navigation station was outfitted with two plush chairs for the pilot and his companion.

Before venturing any further, she decided she would wait for Kace. She could hear him whistling below as he moved about the galley. She was leaning on the rail with her chin cupped in her hand taking in the sights and smells of the harbor when a pair of arms slipped around her waist.

"What do you think?" he whispered softly, pulling her lithesome body back to rest next to the hardness of his.

She could feel the tension building up in him as a hand worked its way under her sweater and around to cup a breast, his fingers gently caressing.

"Kace—don't!" she stammered, answering his question forgotten. "Someone will see us!" She began to squirm, which only served to heighten his desire for her. She could feel his protruding hardness as it pressed into her upper thigh. She trembled.

He chuckled into the nape of her neck as he pushed her thick hair aside. His lips caressed her skin causing the chill bumps to ripple her flesh.

"Don't worry," he whispered, "No one can see us, and even if they could, no one gives a damn what we do."

"I know, but I do," she stressed urgently, trapping his hand against her stomach. She refused to let him have free access to her breast any longer. Why hadn't she put on a bra? she wondered wildly. Maybe it seemed to him she was being promiscuous, just asking for his ardent attention.

Kace kissed her gently on the back of the neck before withdrawing his hands and swinging her around to face him. "Maybe you won't get out of it so easily later." His eyes twinkled. "But right now, I need to take care of business and get us away from here."

Much to Courtney's relief, he left her and made his way toward the front of the yacht. He bent to untie one of the ropes that held it fast.

She remained at the rail, one hand gripping the steel pillar to help steady her wobbly legs. With an anxious look over her shoulder, she watched Kace go forward and start the two powerful engines. As he maneuvered the craft out of the slip, she sank down weakly onto one of the cushioned seats, watching the harbor recede swiftly behind them as they clipped across the water.

It was very pleasant sitting there with the brisk wind and sun playing on her face. Her body was impervious to the cool wind. She was still on fire from Kace's all-consuming touch.

Out of the corner of her eye, she watched Kace as he fiddled with the sophisticated instrument panel in front of him. His narrow-fitting jeans and sweatshirt exposed every muscle of his hard body. He appeared controlled and every bit in command of the situation.

"Hey, Courtney," he called, squinting his eyes in her direction. "Come up here and sit beside me." He reached over and patted the vinyl seat across from him.

Breathing deeply, Courtney pushed herself to her feet and strolled with what she hoped was assured indolence toward him.

As she hoisted herself up into the seat, Kace remarked

casually, "You aren't feeling poorly are you?" His gaze scrutinized her face closely.

Courtney nibbled at her lower lip. "No—no, at least I don't think so," she finished hurriedly.

He smiled. "Good, because today is the first of many trips we'll be making on *The Majestic.*" He paused, significantly. "So you need to be tough."

"Explain to me about all those gadgets on the panel," she forced herself to say in a breathless rush, deliberately changing the subject.

Her sudden move to change the subject wasn't lost on him. "Well, let's see now," Kace drawled mockingly. "This is the temperature gauge, this is the auto pilot . . ."

Courtney gave him her undivided attention, pretending not to see the humor lurking in his eyes and in his voice as he gave her in detail the functions of each instrument.

"Now," he exclaimed smiling, "my throat's parched, thanks to that detailed lesson. Why don't you scamper below and get us both something to drink?"

Needing no further urging, Courtney quickly made her way down the steps and into the cabin below. For a few moments, she remained motionless, drawing deep breaths in hopes of controlling her thumping heart. Honestly, she was acting like an idiot, she told herself with a bitter laugh. It was as if she expected Kace to pounce on her any minute. He wasn't about to do that. And she knew it. So why was she acting as skittish as a cat on a hot tin roof? Now was certainly not the time for recriminations and second thoughts. It was too late for that.

Her eyes hurriedly scanned the tiny but ultra-modern kitchen. There was a stove, refrigerator, sink, and even a microwave oven—all the comforts of home, she thought. Venturing to her right, she peeked into the cabin. It too was impressive. Birch paneling lined the walls, enhanced by the wall-to-wall carpeting and matching drapes. Occupying the center of the room was a double bunk bed with all the other furniture built into the wall, allowing for plenty of walking room.

On her way back to the stairs, after grabbing two cups of freshly perked coffee, Courtney glanced in the second cabin. It turned out to be a replica of the other one, only smaller, with twin bunk beds instead of a double one. Each cabin apparently had its own complete bathroom.

Instead of sitting at the pilot's helm, Kace was squatting on the deck fiddling with what looked to Courtney like fishing line for a rod and reel.

"I'd just about given you up for lost. We've almost reached our fishing spot. It's the best saltwater fishing area around these parts." He stood up, bringing the pole with him. "How are you at frying speckled trout? And catching them?" he added with a chuckle.

Courtney wrinkled her nose at him. "Well, to be absolutely truthful, I'm not too good at either." She broke off with a hapless grin.

Kace rolled his eyes heavenward. "Don't say any more. I get the message. But never fear, my dear, Kace McCord won't let us starve. I'll catch and cook you a batch of fish that'll make your mouth water." He cocked his head to one side and grinned. "I'll have you begging for the recipe."

"Mmmm, that does sound good," Courtney confessed, giving her flat stomach a pat. "But it wouldn't if I had to cook it," she added impishly.

"Oh, no! I thought you were kidding me," Kace exclaimed in mock exasperation. "Don't tell me I've fallen for a woman who doesn't like to cook. Didn't anyone ever tell you," he expanded further, "that the way to a man's heart is through his stomach?"

Kace's teasing remark wasn't lost on Courtney. However, she chose to let it slide, thereby not complicating this beautiful day with any type of argument, no matter how slight, if Kace refused to accept the fact that she wasn't about to make any type of commitment.

His only reaction to Courtney's silence was a momentary tightening of his lips. Kace then nonchalantly strode to the front and abruptly slowed the powerful engines to a snail's pace. With the push of a button, he began lowering the anchor.

"Is—is this where we're going to fish?" Her words came out in a halting whisper. But the place where they were anchored instilled that sense of quietness in her. She saw that they were well away from the shore, into deeper waters. There was no human sound around them. The wind and sun were their only companions, and even they seemed to be on their best behavior.

Clutching her fishing rod in her hand, Courtney casually strolled to the side of the yacht and gazed about her. For January, it was uncanny how beautiful the bay water was. It looked inviting enough for a swim, she thought.

They were on the south side of this huge Lake Pontchartrain, as this was the only accessible area in New Orleans for saltwater sports. Although it was called a lake, Pontchartrain was actually a bay connected to the Gulf of Mexico.

Hearing a shuffling sound close behind her, Courtney

whirled around to see Kace bending down over an ice chest.

Its contents made Courtney jerk her head back with a horrified gasp. "What is that?" she asked, practically shouting.

Amusement crinkled the corners of Kace's eyes. "It's our bait," he acknowledged, his face void of all expression.

Courtney eyed him closely, one eyebrow quirked. "You don't honestly expect me to stick my hand down in there—with those creepy crawly things—do you?" The last part came out in a throaty huff.

"Of course," Kace commented blandly. "It's only live shrimp."

Courtney glared at him. "Only live shrimp!" Her voice rose several more octaves. "If you think for one minute I'm going to put my hand in *there*, you're crazy as—"

"Hell, I know," he finished for her, grinning widely. His eyes were literally dancing with unsuppressed mirth. "If you'll move a little closer, I'll show you how it's done. There's really nothing to it. Watch."

Much to Courtney's trepidation, Kace dipped his hand into the chest and scooped up one of the active little creatures. He then proceeded to take the hook on the end of his rod and reel line and ease it through the hard shell on the upper part of the shrimp.

"Now," he declared confidently, "I'm ready to throw this wiggly fellow overboard and catch us a honey of a speck or a sand trout."

Looking behind him, he raised the rod up and back over his head, and with a zip he cast the rod toward the water. The line grazed the top of the wave for a split second and suddenly all that was visible to the naked eye was the cork bobbing up and down in the gentle swelling waves.

"See, there's nothing to it," he grinned proudly. "It's as easy as falling off a log."

"Huh! That's what you think," Courtney responded with a frown banking her features. "If I have to bait my own hook, I think I'll pass. That is, if it's all the same to you," she added with syrupy sweetness.

Kace reached for the other rod. "No way! Every man for himself. Anyway, I need you to help catch our dinner." He paused, deviltry glimmering in his eyes. "After all, if I'm to be the chief cook and bottle washer on this trip, the least you can do is help catch our dinner! Agreed?"

A frown puckered her lips. "Kace, please, don't!"

He shook his head. "This 'Kace, please, don't,'" he mimicked, "won't work. Not this time. Grab a hold, woman. The fish are hungry."

Courtney realized she wouldn't have a moment's peace if she didn't comply with Kace's demand. She guessed it wouldn't kill her to touch the grotesque little creatures, she told herself wryly. Maybe after she got the hang of it it wouldn't be so bad.

Closing her eyes, she reached her hand into the container and came up with a prickly shrimp. Kace's laughter behind her echoed in the wind. She flashed him a hard look before she gritted her teeth and set about threading the shrimp onto the hook. From then on, it was a piece of cake. In a matter of hours, they had filled the extra cooler to capacity with a mixture of both speckled and sand trout.

It gave her a thrill to wrestle with the fish, especially the speckled trout. She learned quickly that they went down fighting. Several times Courtney felt as if her arm had been jerked out of its socket. When a two-pounder hit her line, Kace, much to his delight, had to help her get it in the boat. When Kace finally called a halt, it was none too soon for her. She was so tired she could hardly move. But she felt proud of herself for accomplishing what she had first thought was totally impossible.

Draping an arm casually around Courtney's shoulders, Kace ventured, "Why don't you take yourself below and indulge in a hot shower. It'll make you feel better." He squeezed her close for a second. "As soon as I finish cleaning the fish, I'll start dinner."

"Sounds good to me," she acquiesced, wearily brushing her windblown hair out of her face. "But don't you really want me to help with dinner?"

Kace flashed her a wicked glance and laughed softly. "Not on your life, honey. Anyway, in your condition, you'd only be underfoot."

"Well . . . if you're sure?"

"I'm sure," he chuckled softly. "Just go get your shower."

As the hot water pounded the soreness out of her shoulders and arms, Courtney felt new life return to her limbs. She felt a twinge of guilt for relaxing in the shower for so long, while Kace was still working. But she brushed the thought aside as quickly as it came to her. He was used to fishing and she wasn't.

While she was drying her body with a big towel, the smell of fried fish tantalized her nose. Then her stomach began to make a low rumbling sound. She was hungry.

Courtney had just donned a clean pair of jeans and

sweater and was brushing her hair when a faint tap on the door halted her actions. "Are you decent?" Kace asked.

"Yes, come on down," she answered.

Kace eased his lanky frame through the small opening and into the room. "My, but something sure smells good," he laughed huskily, taking several deep breaths.

Courtney flushed. "It's—it's just my bath powder, I suppose." Would there ever come a time, she wondered briefly, when his soft-hearted compliments wouldn't catch her off guard? "Did you—uh—want me to do something after all?" she added hesitantly.

His eyes darkened before he cleared his throat. "Yes, I thought maybe you'd watch the French fries while I take a quick shower."

"I'll be right there," she replied briskly. She laid down her brush and patted her hair in place. A swipe of gloss across her chapped lips and she was satisfied with her appearance.

When Courtney walked into the galley, she noticed that Kace had already set the table. A smile crossed her lips at his thoughtfulness. A platter of fish, cut up into small pieces and fried to a golden-brown crispness was sitting in the middle of the stove. The potatoes were sizzling in the same deep skillet where he had fried the fish.

By the time she had a platter heaping full of the delicious potatoes, Kace made his appearance. The clean rich aroma of his cologne that clung to him made her achingly aware of his presence. His silver hair was still damp from his shower and rather unruly. He had put on a pair of slim-legged khakis and a T-shirt. She could see his muscles straining against the thin fabric.

All of a sudden, the cabin seemed too small. The

atmosphere was almost claustrophobic in its intensity. She could feel it, and she knew he could too by the way he held her paralyzed under his glittering gaze.

Her breath caught in her throat and her eyelids fluttered, but she didn't move—couldn't move.

"Don't look so frightened. Right now, the only thing that's on my mind is food," he lied glibly.

Courtney felt again at a loss for words at his uncanny ability to read her mind. But she had to admit that fright was not the most prevalent emotion she was experiencing at this moment, but another one, much more potent.

"How about some wine?" Kace said, abruptly. He reached for a chilled bottle inside the refrigerator and proceeded to uncork it. He then filled two glasses and held the chair out for her.

Tension hovered over the room like a blanket of wet sand. While she sipped on the wine, Kace loaded their plates with fish and potatoes and joined her at the table. A gentle smile curved his lips as he watched her over the rim of his wineglass. "Eat up, before it gets cold," he told her, breaking the silence.

The fish was delicious. The strenuous activity of this afternoon had made them both ravenously hungry.

She helped Kace clear the table and was fumbling unnecessarily with the dirty dishes when instinct and smell, not sight, told her Kace was standing close behind her. There was no time to voice her opposition to his presence, or to move an inch. The moment his hands touched down on her shoulders, Courtney froze.

She was powerless to offer any resistance as he slowly turned her around and pinned her close against his upper body. The side of her cheek lay nestled against his chest where she could feel the prickle of his wiry hair.

A shudder ran through her body as Kace began massaging her back with his large calloused hand. The silence deepened with each passing moment. Kace's erratic breathing was the only sound in the cabin. It made Courtney realize that if she intended to call a halt to his actions it had better be now, or it would be too late.

"Kace," she murmured, trying to wedge a hand between them. "Please, let me go—"

"Let you go!" he groaned, burying his face in her black curls. "I can't. Not this time. I have to hold you, touch you."

"No—" She was having dificulty breathing.

"Yes," he ground out harshly, as his lips began nibbling at the soft area under her ear and then along the side of her neck.

"Oh, Kace," she began achingly.

"Shhh, don't talk, just feel." His warm breath caressed her neck. "Feel how much I need you." He molded her closer against him, leaving no doubt as to his mounting desire for her.

"Kace—I can't, not yet," she whispered through anxiously parted lips.

His mouth silenced her. As his lips worked their magic, she felt her heart almost skid to a complete stop. His kiss was so unbelievably sweet and tender that she found herself frantically fighting to retain control over the situation.

"Courtney, you have to let me love you," he rasped, as his lips left hers. His voice was raw with passion and with longing. "You can't stop me now!"

Courtney's arms slid up around his neck, nothing making any sense anymore, nothing except her need for him. The craving inside her could no longer be denied.

She was hooked—hooked on his silver hair, his warm smile, and his touch.

His lips were crushing hers in another shattering kiss, while his hands were roaming up and down her back leaving a trail of fire everywhere they touched.

Courtney's hunger now matched his. Gone were recriminations, sound reasoning, and common sense. All she cared about was soothing the ache that his hands, his mouth had created. Tomorrow would be soon enough to face reality—but not now, definitely not now.

Kisses fast becoming not enough, Kace swung her off her feet, and carried her toward the large cabin with the double bunk bed.

7

Mouths still clinging, they fell as one on the chenille bedspread. Courtney found herself being buried deeper into the soft mattress as she bore the burden of his hard masculine frame.

With a muffled groan, Kace withdrew his mouth just long enough to change his position. He moved aside and put his hands on her hips, bringing her body into line with his. She felt his need growing against her as she raised her hand to touch his face, his lips with gentle fingers.

"Oh, Courtney, I've dreamed of this moment so many times," he whispered passionately, their lips only a hair's breadth away but not yet touching.

"Me too," she returned shakily.

Needing no further encouragement, his tongue darted out and lightly circled the inside of her lips. At the maddeningly feathery brush of his moist tongue her skin began to tingle.

She opened her mouth, encouraging, welcoming him to seek the hidden treasure that was to be found there. As their mouths clung and tongues sparred, Courtney felt as if her body had ignited in flames.

They moved against each other in a fierce embrace that left her body screaming for more. Clothes were now a cumbersome nuisance, preventing them from discovering the private joys of each other's bodies.

He raised his head and gazed down at her with burning eyes. "Have I ever told you how beautiful you are? How sweet you taste? How desperately I need you?" The timbre of his voice was low and torture ridden.

Courtney stared at him mesmerized by his eyes, his voice. Speech was impossible. She felt something break loose inside of her, something hot and sweet that flooded her limbs and left them trembling.

Her lips parted of their own volition as she sought to receive once again the invasion of his tongue. Clutching her to him, she moaned as his mouth moved suddenly to her ear. His tongue darted into the recess, sending waves of sensation tingling down her neck.

"Kace," she groaned, as she moved her head from side to side to try and counter his arduous assault on her senses.

He continued his advance, now lifting her sweater to plunder the lushness of her body. His hand gently curved around a breast and brought it to pulsating life with gentle stroking and teasing. The nipples became as hard as diamonds under his expert touch.

With a burning need to know and see all of her, Kace began to pull the sweater from her body. The cool air blowing through the cabin's window, when it hit her bare skin, aroused her out of her languor. She watched as he carelessly flung the garment aside, turning to feast his eyes on the satin whiteness of her breasts.

"Oh, Courtney, I love the shape of you," he modulated hoarsely. "You're so lovely." He began to stroke her breasts with fingers as gentle as velvet.

As Courtney lay quivering beneath his practiced touch, the room seemed to be aglow with a kind of magic. Kace's gray hair shone like soft light from the moon, silvering over them.

She reached up to touch the silver mane as if it wasn't real, only to delve her fingers deep into it, as Kace seared her nipples with his hot moist tongue. She gasped her pleasure aloud as the sweet savage agony continued. His adventurous tongue as it made its way around the underside of her breast, downward to her stomach, was almost her undoing.

But when his mouth and tongue encountered the button on her jeans, he muffled a soft curse, and he groped to pull the tight-fitting pants from her hips.

With trembling hands, she joined in the efforts and was soon lying naked before him. The moonlight draped a veil of silvery light over her body, making her appear almost ethereal.

He quickly stood up and removed his own clothes, drinking in the beauty of her body as he did so. Stretching out beside her, he ran loving hands over her perfectly shaped legs, the insides of her thighs, coming to rest for a moment on the flatness of her stomach. His mouth followed the path of his hands. When he caressed her navel with his mouth and then buried his tongue there, she grasped his head, tangling once again her fingers into his hair.

She began to move against him. Excitement and

anticipation caused her breathing to grow shallow and ragged.

"Oh, Kace!" she moaned.

He moved upward with the agility of a cougar and kissed her moist and parted lips.

Kace ached for her. He was desperate to take her, but he had to know she was ready for him. For he wanted their first coupling to be beautiful. To be perfect. To be remembered.

His hands and fingers with silken softness, explored her secret sweetness. Courtney felt a hot liquid course through her at his gentle touch.

Wrenching her mouth from his, Courtney whispered, her voice taut with emotion, "Kace, please—take me!" She wanted him. Now. She wanted to feel him inside of her. To know and feel what it was like to be truly loved by a man.

His obsession for her in that moment overcame all else. He, too, could wait no longer to take what she was so freely offering.

Gently, he stroked her legs apart and then moved over her. He brought his lips to her breasts and tasted their sweetness once more before completing the last stage of their sensuous journey.

Cautiously he entered her and began slow measured thrusts. Courtney felt herself drowning in the wonderment of it all. Impatient for all of him, she grabbed his shoulders for support and arched herself against him.

"Courtney, no!" Kace rasped as his thrusting force met a surprising barrier.

"Please, don't stop. Not now. It's all right," she whispered urgently as she stroked his face, drawing him closer to her.

He groaned and quickened his thrusts and soon found himself nestled completely within her satin folds. From there the pace slowed with each move bringing her past the pain and into a world of erotic delight.

"Yes, yes, yes," she heard herself whisper, as her hips tilted to meet his, driving him deeper and deeper into her softness.

A shiver of wild delight washed over her as together they reached the heights of ecstasy. Afterward, he moaned as he buried his face into her hair that was spread on the pillow.

The room was still—except for the pounding of their hearts. Tentatively, Courtney turned and kissed his hand that lay resting against her cheek. Then she touched his shoulder with her tongue. Although his body was moist with perspiration, it tasted delicious.

Soon, she felt him relax completely. He rolled over on his side and took her with him. No words were spoken as he kissed her lips tenderly. Their mouths finally separating, he smoothed her damp hair away from her face and stared down into the shimmering softness of her eyes. With a sigh, he drew her head down to rest in the crook of his arm, listening to the accelerated beating of her heart.

Although his heart had ceased its pounding, his mind had not. His thoughts raced madly. A virgin! He still couldn't believe she had been totally untouched by a man. But she had satisfied him so. And he was so deeply delighted by her. She was different, so completely unlike other women he'd known. Naive in the nicest way and yet gentle in her giving.

He sighed as he held her slight body close against him. He never wanted to let her go. Even now, as he held her, he felt his insides quiver from wanting to repeat what had taken place between them. He longed to show her, free of pain, how it was to love and be loved.

Courtney lay in a dreamy state of contentment. She, too, hated to move for fear of breaking the spell of enchantment surrounding them.

She felt him swing his leg gently over hers, pinning her partially under him once more.

"Did I hurt you?" he asked softly, uncertainty lacing his voice.

"No. It was wonderful," she responded softly.

A deep silence followed her words.

"Why didn't you tell me you'd never known a man?" he chastised mildly.

"You—you never asked me." Her voice held a tremor.

He sighed. "I should have known. But you responded so ardently to my every move . . ." His voice trailed off.

"I guess that proves what a good teacher you are."

He chuckled as his leg began a patient but intent movement up and down her thigh.

"It helps to have a willing pupil. And I can honestly say your body was meant for the pleasures of loving a man." His voice had grown hoarse, raspy.

"I'm—I'm glad I pleased you," she whispered gently.

"Oh, honey," he groaned raggedly, "you are absolutely perfect."

He turned her face slightly toward him and moved his lips against hers. His hands had replaced his leg and were causing strange shooting sensations throughout her body. She felt her nipples harden in anticipation of his brazen touch. Wandering fingers surveyed the softness of her stomach and then sought the rounded curves of her hips only to delve lower to her vault of velvet.

From his feathery strokes, she felt her own passion rise anew. She was determined to join in the passion play this time. She let her hands move by their own accord, lower and lower, exploring his body, calling his name.

She felt him swell and rise to the occasion. She gasped as his mouth found her nipples, drawing on the sweetness he found there. Then, he rolled her onto her back, entered her gently, and began the slow, delicious movement again.

This time their bodies fit together like pieces of an ancient puzzle. As they moved, Courtney surrendered herself to a fiery flood of sensations that coursed through her. They both shuddered at the same time and floated from heaven back to earth.

They lay spent, wrapped in each other's arms for a timeless moment before he moved from her. Immediately he pulled her close again, pressing the length of her exhausted body against his.

With his hands at her breast, she heard his breath become measured and deep. She knew he had fallen into a deep sleep.

Too tired to wonder or to think about the change that had just taken place in her life, Courtney covered their moist bodies with a sheet and drifted into a dreamless sleep to the steady lapping of waves against the yacht.

The same movement that had rocked Courtney to sleep awakened her late the next morning. Without moving, she slowly opened her eyelids to stare at the tiny clock beside the bed, proving the lateness of the hour. Instinct told her that the place beside her was now empty.

Then with the speed of the wink of an eye, the whole of last night came thundering down upon her. Barely breathing, a sharp pain stabbed at her heart. She turned and saw Kace standing at the porthole, his back to her. Although the morning seemed quite chilly, he was clad only in his jeans. Courtney took in the wide expanse of his bare muscled back as he stood quietly, obviously lost in his own thoughts. He was totally unaware of her scrutiny.

In the clear light of dawn she wondered what he was thinking. Hot tears pricked her eyes as she continued her perusal of him. She had given her virginity to this strong and virile man, something she didn't think she was capable of ever doing. Was she sorry? No. She had wanted him. She would admit that. In all these years, he was the only man that had been able to make her body and her emotions respond.

Could this all-consuming feeling she had for him be love? Was it possible that she was actually in love with him? Love? Was the fact she needed and wanted him like she wanted and needed the breath to live, be love? But could it be possible for her to actually love a man she had known such a short time? Her heart raced madly at the thought.

What of him? Now that the chase was over, now that he had broken through her defenses, would the game be over? Would today be the end of their time together? No. Somehow she didn't think so. She knew he found her attractive and enjoyed making love to her. But even in the throes of passion, he had never committed himself to her.

As these thoughts screamed silently through her mind, she was pressed not to cry out her frustration. Instead, she moved, though slightly. It was enough, however, to draw his attention. He turned rather abruptly to look at her, a frown knitting his brows together.

"How long have you been awake?" he ventured huskily.

"Not long," she admitted, averting her gaze.

"Courtney," he demanded softly, "look at me."

She pressed her lips together as she forced herself to look at him. She endeavored to present a calm facade.

Kace sighed heavily as he took in the faintly bruised shadows under her eyes. His voice became grim. "Courtney, I want us to get married. Immediately. This afternoon, if possible. If not, then tomorrow morning for sure."

Courtney was flabbergasted! She stared at him round-eyed and confused. She clutched the sheet tightly in her hand and drew it closer to her as if it would offer her protection. A proposal of marriage was the last thing she had expected from him. Her brain was working furiously as she tried to assimilate what it might mean.

When Courtney found her voice, she clipped, "You're kidding!" She felt goose bumps crawl over her skin at this frightening change of events.

Kace didn't move. A muscle working in his jaw was the only outward visibility of his agitation. His tone, however, left nothing to the imagination. His words fell like chips of ice between them.

"Courtney, I told you once before that I don't issue idle invitations or make idle statements," he reproved in a deadly calm voice. "I say what I mean and mean what I say, so never make the mistake of doubting me again."

Her reaction to his words was twofold: hurt and anger pierced her heart at the same time. She felt like a cornered animal being lured into a cage for which there would be no escape. Her mind and heart both rebelled in that instant. She would admit that yes, she had been ready for the physical mating with Kace. But a mental commitment was something else, again.

Even though she might love him, she still couldn't face marriage or the responsibility to it. She still had her career and her lifestyle. As far as she was concerned, marriage wouldn't fit well into either.

Anyway, hadn't he merely asked her to marry him because he felt a sense of guilt at having taken her virginity? The word *love* had yet to cross his lips. There was no way she would ever create ties that bound her to a man who didn't love her. She simply couldn't risk getting hurt all over again. This time she had much more to lose.

Her life suited her just fine the way it was. She certainly didn't need a conscience-ridden proposal from this man or any other. She was perfectly capable of accepting the responsibility of her actions of last night and living with them. Wasn't she?

"Courtney, you've got to listen to me!"

His demanding voice broke into her reverie; she had trouble reorienting herself in order to answer him.

She shook her head firmly, causing the disarray of tangled curls to shadow her face. "No, Kace," she admonished. "I don't have to listen to you. I only have to listen to myself. The answer is no. I cannot and will not marry you."

His body stiffened as if indeed she had dealt him a low blow. She could see the battle raging within him and knew beyond a shadow of a doubt that he was hanging onto his temper by a thread.

Slowly expelling his breath, Kace stated simply: "Okay then, if you won't marry me, we'll just have to live together." He ignored the strangled sound coming from her throat, and continued. "I want it understood up front, though, that this isn't my first choice." He paused flatly, watching her cool eyes with a kind of hunger. "But I'll take you any way I can get you, marriage or no marriage."

Her lips began to tremble. She didn't know what to say or do next. Her thoughts were in a turmoil as he stalked her like a panther trying to force her into making a decision.

Kace stood with his hand jammed into his pockets and hooded eyes watched her with calculated appraisal. He was like an unmovable object.

Courtney felt her heart turn over at how near and dear he was to her. Some of the best moments of her life had been those she had spent in his arms. Thinking about the delights his hands and tongue had shown her rekindled a hunger within her now. So why couldn't she reach out and take what he was offering? Here was her chance to have him without the strangling ties of commitment. Was her hesitation because she knew he didn't love her? She couldn't quite identify the emotion that held her silent, but whatever it was, it had a grip on her that wouldn't let go.

"Kace, I—"

"Please," he cut in swiftly, "before you say no, I promise there'll be no pressures, no ties." He smiled as he covered the short distance between them and lowered himself on the foot of the bed.

"No, Kace," she told him firmly. She must make him accept her answer. Now. Before she had time to weaken. "Why can't we leave things the way they are for now? I'm not ready—I can't—I need more time—I—" She felt hot tears prick her eyes as she floundered for the right words to try and make him understand her feelings, her insecurities.

Kace's harsh indrawn breath filled the tiny cabin. When he finally spoke his voice was low and terse. "For God's sake, Courtney, how much more time do you need?"

"I—I don't know. I just need time, that's all," she pleaded. Her eyes, big as saucers, were shimmering with unshed tears.

For a split second, Kace was tempted to go with his gut instinct and grab her and shake some sense into her hard head. It was all he could do to keep his hands off her. But he knew, with certainty, he would only frighten her more and only increase his own agony by driving her further away from him.

So it was with a heavy heart that Kace answered her. "All right, Courtney, for now, we'll play it your way." His mouth became oddly twisted. "It seems this is becoming a way of life with us—me pulling and you pushing." He expelled a deep sigh. "Maybe I can keep it up a little longer." His last words were spoken more to himself than to her. He sounded as if he was trying to convince himself as well as her that he would be able to wait her out.

A dark inscrutable mask slipped over his face as he continued speaking in a tense voice. "Under the circumstances, I think we'd better leave and return to New Orleans, don't you?"

It was shortly after one o'clock when *The Majestic* sailed into the harbor at Lake Pontchartrain.

Courtney had expected the homeward journey to be carried out in strained silence, but to her amazement it wasn't. Kace had reverted back to his usual smiling and urbane self. Although he went out of his way not to touch her, he teased and flirted with her just the same.

But she wasn't fooled by his veneer of tranquility and charm. She knew underneath there was a core of steel and determination to match. He had lost only one battle. He had no intention of losing the war. She knew he wasn't giving up—that he would fight to the bitter end to make her his.

Courtney felt herself shiver. She knew time was running out for her. Kace wouldn't be content to play the game by her rules for much longer. No matter what he promised.

"What's wrong?" Kace asked softly, breaking into her thoughts. "Are you cold?"

Shrugging off her premonitions of doom, she turned to him with a smile.

"A little," she admitted. "It looks like the bottom is going to fall out of the sky any minute now." Her gaze encompassed the cloudy void above them while Kace competently maneuvered the yacht into its slip.

Courtney breathed a sigh of relief when she found herself safely in the Mercedes. As she waited for Kace to take care of the small details concerning the harboring of the yacht, she watched the lightning dance across the sky. Although it was early afternoon, it looked like twilight instead. The sky was becoming darker with each passing moment.

As Kace made a mad dash for the car, the rain began pelting down. He managed to escape getting drenched by a split second.

"Whew!" he exclaimed as he lowered his gangly frame behind the wheel. "Something tells me that if we'd stayed out there any later we'd have been in big trouble." He flashed her a grin as he turned on the ignition.

"Are you going to be able to drive in all this?" she inquired, her brows puckering in a concerned frown.

"Well, I can see fine right now," he replied confidently. Courtney could see his knuckles tighten as he concentrated on keeping the car from skidding on the slippery pavement. "But," he added, "if it gets any worse, I'll be forced to pull over and wait until it slacks up."

Courtney decided it would be best not to distract him by carrying on an idle conversation, so she remained quiet with her hands clasped tightly in her lap.

By the time they reached her condominium, her nerves were in shreds. The rain had abated somewhat, but the sky still rocked with thunder and lightning. Courtney hated storms and even more so when she was forced to endure them in a vehicle.

"Well, we might as well make a run for it," Kace told her with a frown plaguing his features. "It doesn't look like it's even thinking about stopping." He paused, searching the sky. "At least not any time soon, that is."

"Oh, Kace, no! We'll get drenched," she wailed in protest at his suggestion.

He threw her a grin. "So?"

She glared at him. "Getting soaked isn't my favorite pastime, you know," she bit out sarcastically.

"Oh, gee, Courtney. I'm sorry," he apologized. "I had no idea you'd melt. Please, forgive me."

For a moment Courtney was taken aback. Then she saw the smile as it threatened to erupt from his lips. His eyes danced merrily.

Realizing how silly she sounded, her features broke

into a rather sheepish grin. "All right, I concede. You've made your point, you devil. Just lead the way."

Her comment drew a hearty chuckle from him. "I've been called many things in my day, but the devil is a new one on me."

"Oh, really," she remarked smoothly, cocking her head to one side. "I happen to think it fits you to a T."

He laughed. "Well, I always say, if the shoe fits, wear it."

Before Courtney could make a suitable rejoinder, Kace was out of the car and bolting around to her side to help her out. Together, they scooted the short distance to her front door and inside.

There was a moment's silence as they shook the water off.

"Oh, damn," Kace muttered, breaking into the quietness. "I nearly forgot. We're supposed to attend Mark and Juli's party at the country club this evening. It's business mixed with pleasure concerning the China deal."

Courtney's brows furrowed. "Surely not in this weather?"

"I'm hoping it's only a cold front blowing through that's triggering the bad weather. Maybe a little later, after it passes through, things will clear up a bit." He paused momentarily, as he took in the delightful picture she made with her scrubbed rosy-cheeked appearance and the wet blue-black curls clinging softly to her face. He coughed as if to clear his throat before continuing. "Anyway, I'd hate to disappoint them at this late date."

Courtney shrugged. "Are you positive it's still on for this evening?"

"Probably so," he acknowledged, "if I know Juli. I'll tell you what, if you don't hear from me shortly be ready by eight. Okay?"

She sighed. "In that case, you'd better go and let me get busy. I have a lot to do."

"Nothing like being shown the door," he teased lightly. He made his exit, nonetheless, with a slight caress to her cheek and a quick "see you later" thrown over his shoulder.

The next few hours found Courtney working like a Trojan in order to be ready by the appointed time. After being around salt water for the past two days, her skin felt unduly rough and dry. So she took extra time and effort with her toilette. Instead of taking her usual shower, she chose to take a leisurely bath, encasing herself in bubbles up to her neck. As she toweled her sweetly scented body, a weakness invaded her limbs at the thought of how she had given herself to Kace with utter abandonment. Nothing had remained sacred as they sought to learn the hidden joys of each other's bodies.

After taking a moment to regroup her thoughts, Courtney channeled her energy into making herself presentable. Her hair after vigorous shampooing and drying cascaded in soft allure around her face and neck.

By the time the doorbell chimed at one minute of eight, Courtney felt she looked her very best. She had chosen to wear what she hoped would be appropriate for the occasion. It was a full-skirted dress made of white featherweight wool with long sleeves and a plunging neckline. After slipping into it and looping the buttons at the back of the waistline, she whirled in front of the full-length mirror one last time.

Was the neckline too provocative? she wondered as

she surveyed the overall effect. No, she decided, definitely not. She felt there would be others there dressed much more daringly than she. Anyway, the soft wool caressing her skin felt good as she walked, showing off to perfection the hint of bare skin.

When she opened the door to admit Kace, she knew she had chosen well. He didn't have to say a word, his eyes said it all. A bright blaze leapt into them as he devoured her. She saw the Adam's apple in his throat jump as he swallowed trying to find his voice.

She smiled sweetly as she stepped aside allowing him to enter. She, too, thought he was equally as pleasing to the eye in a gray suit with dress shirt to match. The color blended with his silver hair to create a stunning combination.

After closing the door behind him, their eyes met and held. The warm admiration radiating from his dark eyes reached out and wrapped itself around her like a second skin.

In a husky voice, deep with feeling, he murmured, "You're more beautiful than I ever thought possible."

8

~~~~~~~~~~~~~~~~~~~~~~~

When they arrived at the exclusive Woodlake country club a short time later, Courtney noted several cars were already there.

Lights poured from every window of the stately mansion, showing off to perfection its two-storied splendor. As Kace escorted her up the long sidewalk, they could hear the music floating out the windows.

Courtney took one last breath of the fresh oxygen before stepping into what she knew would be an overcrowded situation. She was prepared to encounter the usual stale cigarette smoke that went hand in hand with these kind of functions. As she inhaled deeply, she realized Kace had been right in his weather forecast. Not too long after he had left her, the rain had ceased, leaving in its wake cold wind. Now the wind was no longer stirring, which made for a beautiful and clear evening.

A manservant took her wrap as they entered a room filled with laughter and beautiful people. It was still early, so the cigarette smoke wasn't yet offensive. Courtney joined Kace as he led her around the room greeting friends and making introductions. They still hadn't located the host and hostess, which Courtney thought was a little unusual.

They made their way toward the bar located in the corner of the huge room where the majority of the people were gathered. Courtney saw Mark Davidson's smiling face as he strode hastily toward them.

"I'm sorry, friend," he apologized, clapping Kace on the back and giving Courtney a swift peck on the cheek, "but Juli had me in the kitchen working on the icemaker. Would you believe the darned thing just quit on us a little while ago?" He smiled ruefully. "I just now got it working again."

"That's all right, Mark. I wasn't worried. I knew you'd show up sooner or later," Kace expressed with a smile. "Where's your wife? She's the one I really want to see."

Mark grinned. "She's scurrying around here somewhere." His eyes searched the room. "She's probably at the refreshment table making sure the 'goodies' are kept replenished. Come on," he motioned, "let's get you two a drink and then we'll head that way."

Taking Courtney by the arm, Mark whispered close to her ear but loud enough for Kace to hear, "You look absolutely stunning in that dress, Courtney. If I weren't a happily married man, I'd give Kace here a run for his money." He grinned broadly as he squeezed her arm.

"Not on your life, you young whippersnapper." Kace paused to draw Courtney back against his side. "This classy lady belongs exclusively to me." Although he smiled, Courtney heard the steel that always surfaced in his voice when he wished to get a point across.

"Sounds good to me," laughed Mark. "I'd be the last one to argue with that."

Before Courtney could take offense at Kace's bold statement, a pretty blonde approached them with a broad smile on her face.

"Well, Kace McCord," she exclaimed enthusiastically, "it's about time you showed up. I'd despaired of ever seeing you again."

"Ah now, Juli, you know better than that. You know I wouldn't desert my best girl," Kace averred, a smile tugging at the corners of his mouth.

"Well, I just wanted to make sure," she responded with a grin. "But whatever you've been up to, it agrees with you. You're looking great!"

Draping his arm around Juli's shoulders, Kace turned toward Courtney and said, "Honey, I'd like for you to meet Mark's better half, Juli. Juli, this is Courtney Roberts."

"Hello, Courtney," the blonde acknowledged with warm politeness. "I'm so glad you could come to the party." She paused to look up at her husband, giving him a half-rueful smile. "Although I'm not sure how much of a party it really is. I've been reminded several times that a certain few of the men will have to leave the women for a while in order to tend to a little business." She rolled her eyes upward as she stressed the word *little*.

"Now, sweetheart," Mark grinned as he tenderly drew his wife close to his side and kissed her on the temple. "I promised I'd keep the meeting short and sweet, didn't I?"

"You can bet it won't take long," Kace chimed in forcefully. "If I have anything to say about it, that is!"

"Bully for you," Juli stated with a laugh. "I'm going to hold you to that."

Juli Davidson, Courtney realized, reminded her very much of Amy, not in looks, but rather in personality. They were both warm and witty. Although Juli's features were plain, her wide-spaced brown eyes and blond hair made for an overall attractive package. She laughed often, and there was a certain something about her that drew people to her like a magnet. And it was obvious that she and Mark were crazy about each other. Next to their happiness, her lifestyle paled in comparison, she thought with a strange pang.

"Would you like to sit down?" Kace's soft tone cut gently into her reverie. Courtney and Kace, along with Juli and Mark and several other couples, made their way into the plush lounging area adjacent to the party room. Names were bounced around casually, and after a while she gave up trying to put names with faces. One middle-aged couple Kace did point out to her as being important was Simon and Kay Falkner. Mr. Falkner, he told her, was the instigator of the China deal.

The atmosphere was one of gaiety and general camaraderie as they discussed everything from the sagging economy, to world affairs, and then back to the losing season of the New Orleans Saints.

Courtney was content to sit and listen to the good-natured arguments and not take part in the conversation. More than anything else, she was extremely conscious of Kace's body pressed close to her own as they were jammed next to each other on the couch.

The warmth of his thigh against her leg seared through her clothing as it continually massaged her with his every move. His long fingers resting only inches from her hand, made her long to reach out and touch them. It suddenly rankled her that she should find life incomplete unless she could reach out her hand and touch him in some small way.

His mental telepathy apparently at work again, Kace's hand snaked out and gently gave hers a gentle squeeze, before turning to answer a question someone threw at him. Courtney felt her heart flip-flop at his sudden action. She observed him as he continued to laugh and enjoy his friends. He was relaxed and vibrated a magnetism that was felt and accepted by everyone in the group.

It was a short time later that Mark held up his hand, halting the conversation. "It's time, I believe, Kace, for us to excuse ourselves and get the business out of the way," he announced. "Anyway, I'm itching to get back and do some dancing!"

This drew laughter from around the circle as the men rose to take their leave.

Kace leaned down and whispered in Courtney's ear, "I won't be long, honey. Juli'll take care of you."

For the next couple of hours, Courtney thoroughly enjoyed Juli's company and constant chatter. She learned that she and Mark had two small daughters, only fourteen months apart. She also learned that until she and Kace began seeing each other, Kace was a constant visitor to their house.

Juli rounded off that statement with a confession. "Both Mark and I have been pushing Kace toward settling down again." She paused, cocking her head sideways. "According to the man in question, he's ready to do just that." Her smile deepened. "Apparently, he's found the right woman."

Courtney, much to her dismay, felt her cheeks flush with color at Juli's gentle ribbing. Her reaction brought a burst of laughter and a "knowing" look from the petite blonde, but no more personal revelations followed, much to Courtney's relief. She was beginning to feel stifled and pressured from all the talk of "settling down."

As Juli made her rounds as a hostess, Courtney followed, helping where she could to keep the party moving and the guests happy.

Courtney had strolled to the buffet table herself and was sampling the hors d'oeuvres, the canapés, and other tidbits when she looked up and saw Kace making his way, undeterred, toward her.

He smiled. "Let me get some of this delicious-looking stuff, and we'll sneak off somewhere quiet and gorge ourselves." His smile widened into a grin making the lines beneath his cheeks crease even deeper, accenting the strength of his face.

Courtney nodded and answered his grin with one of her own, thinking anew how ruggedly handsome he was and determined! *Oh, how determined,* she thought with an inner sigh.

With heaping plates, Kace guided her gently, his hand on her elbow back to the living room. This time they were lucky enough to have it to themselves; most of the guests were either eating or dancing. They sat down silently and began immediately to eat.

Setting her plate on the table, Courtney turned toward Kace and smiled. "Was the meeting successful?" she asked casually.

His lips mirrored her smile. "Very much so. When we

sign on the dotted line, the China deal will be in our pocket."

"I'm glad," she expressed warmly.

"What do you think about Juli?" he asked, changing the subject. His eyes as they probed hers were slightly hooded.

"I liked her on sight," Courtney replied promptly.

"I thought you might. Juli's a fine person, and she and Mark are very happy together," he added mildly.

Courtney remained silent, swallowing her irritation brought on by his words. Did he, she wondered, bring her to this party in order to flaunt his friends' happy marriage in front of her? The thought nagged at her for a minute, but deciding she was being ridiculous even thinking such a thing, she dismissed it.

The silence deepened between them as they watched the other couples take part in various merrymaking activities. Some danced frantically, moving in time to the rock music the band was playing. While others, like them, sat in small groups drinking, and laughing.

Suddenly, Courtney felt Kace staring at her, his gaze warmly penetrating. She felt the old familiar tingling sensation in the pit of her stomach.

"Will you dance with me?" he asked, the tone of his voice husky, intimate.

Not waiting for her consent, Kace stood up and reached for her hand, pulling her up beside him. As their bodies made casual contact, Courtney felt her nipples harden in response.

On shaky legs, she allowed Kace to lead her the short distance to the dance floor. He drew her to him immediately, molding her against the hard contours of his body.

As the music had now slowed, Kace adjusted his

movements to keep perfect time to the sensuous rhythm. Courtney felt the heat that generated from his body actually burn through both their clothing, searing her skin.

This was the first time Courtney had ever danced with Kace. It was a completely new experience for her. His body continued to move in cat-like grace as they swayed as one to the music. Courtney felt as if her heart would burst from the sheer force of his vibrant smell and his masculine closeness.

Even though words remained unspoken between them, Kace's body and eyes talked for him. When she looked up into his face, she saw a naked passion mirrored there. Courtney caught her breath in a gasp and in doing so parted her lips, anticipating the fitting sweetness of his.

But the kiss never materialized, leaving Courtney filled with a desolate longing. Instantly, the music had switched from easy listening to rock. Kace drew back with a shudder at the total and abrupt change in the mood. Tight-lipped, he released her and guided her back to the table.

Their unfinished drinks were waiting for them, and Courtney latched on to hers like a lifeline, trying to soothe the parched dryness of her throat and calm her frayed nerves. Why, she wondered, for perhaps the thousandth time, did Kace's touch affect her like a lighted match to a stick of dynamite? This whole affair was beginning to get out of hand. She really felt she was no longer in full control of her emotions, and it frightened her.

Tension claimed the air between them as they sat silent, each lost in his own thoughts.

A short time later, after glasses were empty, Kace spoke. "Now that I've gotten the business out of the way and you've met Juli, I'm ready to go, how about you?" There was a sensual glow in his eyes as they eagerly appraised her.

Courtney nodded, her voice too full to speak. A promise of what was surely to follow their departure caused waves of desire to leap through the lower half of her body.

In her state of euphoria, she said her goodbyes to Mark and Juli, promising to keep in touch, and allowed Kace to lead her toward the Mercedes, one arm firmly around her waist. The night air had grown chiller, making Courtney breathe a sigh of relief when she found herself warmly cocooned in the car.

Courtney's inflamed senses were her silent companion as Kace guided the car onto the busy intersection. She felt them grow stronger as they approached her condominium. His silence and the tenseness of his expression proved that he, too, felt the emotional charge that buzzed between them.

Very soon, she thought, she would feel his arms around her and his lips on her body.

When they reached the front door, Courtney gave him the key. Once the door was opened, she started to cross the threshold but then stopped abruptly on hearing his words.

"Good night, Courtney. I'll call you tomorrow." He leaned down and brushed his lips across hers.

Courtney clasped the key he dangled in front of her with trembling fingers. She managed to force the words *good night* through stiffened lips as she stood still as a mummy and stared at his retreating back in puzzled amazement.

It seemed eons before she closed the door and made her way into the bedroom. The sense of uncertainty concerning Kace's behavior was growing deeper with each passing minute. Was this his way of showing her that he was indeed backing off—giving her more time? she wondered. After all he had promised not to pressure her. But what of his behavior at the party? He didn't act as if he had any intention of giving up. Instead of feeling relief at this sudden and new turn of events, she felt slightly miffed. Her body still harbored the need to know his touch. The fire had definitely been banked but not extinguished. Her desire lay smoldering, and, as a result, she went to bed with an aching void inside her.

The next day Kace did call her as promised and every day thereafter as the month of February zipped by with amazing speed. If Courtney wasn't conversing with Kace on the phone, she was with him at least four out of the seven nights a week. But there was definitely a difference in his attitude toward her.

Although he treated her with the same gentle courtesy and warmth as always, he never once tried to entice her to share his bed. It was almost as if their passion-filled night on the yacht had never happened. She was at a loss as to how to handle the abrupt change in their relationship. It was as if they had reached an impasse. And it constantly nagged at her, his determination to keep his promise not to push her. Could he by any chance be losing interest in her? She asked herself this question over and over.

Then on Valentine's Day he surprised her with a beautiful dainty gold and diamond necklace. She opened the box, and, for a moment, she was completely robbed of her voice. Her first thought was to refuse the gift because of its connotations. But the look on Kace's face changed her mind. He was as excited and eager as a small child seeing Santa for the first time. Deciding to give him the benefit of the doubt, she smilingly accepted the necklace. If bribery was his intention, he had fallen far short of his goal, she told herself proudly.

Courtney saw the arrival of March with Kace still behaving in much the same manner. On the surface, he was determined; but there was a certain part of himself he held aloof. Courtney's confusion was growing with each passing day.

On Friday afternoon, the first of March, the telephone rang at Paper-Work-Plus. It was Kace.

"Are you about to close up for the day?" he asked cheerfully.

"As a matter of fact I was," Courtney returned lightly. "Why?"

He chuckled. His voice sounded warm and deep over the phone, causing her pulse to accelerate, much to her annoyance.

"Because I'm going to treat you to another deliciously prepared dinner by none other than Chef McCord." He paused. "Can I expect you by seven-thirty?"

Courtney's mouth went dry. "All—all right. I'll be there."

"See you then," he said, his voice bordering on laughter and something else. Was it mockery? she wondered, as she held the dead receiver a moment before putting it down. She wished she knew what kind of cat-and-mouse game he was playing.

Arriving home shortly thereafter, Courtney took a shower and then pondered what to wear. Comfort was the deciding factor in choosing a red outfit made of a soft fabric that had the texture of silk. The lines were simple, making it appropriate for any occasion. It was also suitable to be worn without a bra. Any time she was permitted the freedom of doing without the confining garment, she took advantage of it.

Kace was smiling broadly when he opened the door to admit her. He looked great in a pair of dark slacks, which hinted at the muscular power of his thighs, and a pale yellow knit shirt.

"Something smells delicious!" she exclaimed, wrinkling her nose but at the same time trying to combat the forces of his attraction.

"But not nearly as delicious as you look," he grinned, running his blue eyes appreciably over her ebony curls, down the entire length of her body. "Red is definitely your color."

"Thank you," she murmured hastily as she swept past him and made her way toward the dining room.

The table was beautifully decorated, complete with fine crystal and candles. This elaborate display was so out of character for Kace that she didn't try to mask her astonishment.

"Well, I'm waiting for the compliment. Let's have it!" he pressed softly from close behind her.

"It's—it's lovely," she answered truthfully. "But I don't understand." She took a step forward and then turned to look at him, a disconcerted frown on her face. "What's the occasion?"

Kace shrugged. "Nothing really. I just thought you could use a good meal." He paused, reaching out a finger and gently rubbing it across the dusky spots underneath her eyes. "I know for a fact you've had a hard week. I'm trying my best to keep you healthy."

Courtney felt a sweet yearning shoot through her body at his tender touch and his thoughtfulness. Was this man to remain an enigma to her forever? she wondered despairingly. When she thought she had him figured out, he would pull the unexpected.

"I hope you like lasagna," he remarked, breaking into her musings. "I've been up to my elbows in noodles and ricotta cheese nearly all afternoon," he went on to admit with a sheepish grin. "But it's absolutely fantastic, even if I do say so myself!"

And it was. Everything was perfect—the crisp garden salad, the lasagna, the pull-apart bread, and the red wine which accompanied the meal. They both ate with a hearty appetite, feeling no need to make idle conversation to interfere with the comfortable silence. Later Kace did invite her to join him, his daughter, and son-in-law shopping for antiques in the French Quarter the next day, to be followed that night by dinner at a club. He added that Susan wanted to get her shopping done before the celebration of Mardi Gras began the following Tuesday. To this invitation, Courtney promptly gave her acceptance, never passing up a chance to seek out the hidden treasures that were so much a part of the old town of New Orleans.

After turning down Kace's offer of apple strudel for dessert, Courtney sighed with deep contentment as she watched Kace refill their wineglasses, strongly conscious of the calm assurance with which he did everything.

Instinctively she glanced up, wanting to share her feelings with him, but suddenly his expression had become rather remote, making it impossible for her to utter a word. Instead she toyed with her wineglass, waiting for him to bridge the gap of silence.

"Let's enjoy our wine in the den, shall we?" he ventured after another prolonged moment, a smile once again lurking around the corners of his mouth.

What were his thoughts when he got that far away, abstracted look in his eyes? Courtney wondered apprehensively.

Although the evening wasn't cold, Kace had built a small fire in the fireplace to take the chill off. It felt good to Courtney as she sat down on the small couch closest to it. Kace followed, lowering himself beside her with their wine in his hands.

He handed Courtney hers, and she silently sipped the mellow liquid and watched the flickering brightness of the flames. Then she turned and found Kace's eyes on her.

"Would you like to hear something on the stereo?"

"Sounds good to me."

He nodded, swallowing his drink. He got up with a jerky movement, crossed the room, and knelt down in front of the massive stereo system that took up the entire wall. Momentarily, the haunting voice of a jazz singer filled the room.

Courtney felt her heart begin to pound in her throat as he made his way back toward her. He appeared to be wound as tight as a bow string, his eyes dark and unreadable.

She bent her head, unknowingly exposing the tender

curve of her nape to his gaze. Courtney adjusted herself to the burden of his weight as he once more occupied the cushion beside her.

He reached out and began to gently massage her shoulder. The soothing motion helped her relax and caused a little of her weariness to disappear.

"Mmmm, that feels so good," she murmured, raising her head only to let it wobble loosely on her neck as he continued to knead the kinks from her muscles.

Kace was right, she admitted to herself, she and Amy had indeed put in another bad week. One of the machines had broken down, and they had been operating one short, which added to the confusion.

She was so lost in her thoughts she wasn't aware when his touch changed from one of tender administering to one of gentle persuasion until she felt his fingers working their same magic on her breast, arousing her nipple to button hardness. His hand soon stilled, and Courtney watched in utter bemusement as Kace lowered his head and laid his lips on hers. It was a tormentingly gentle kiss, prolonged by the locking of Courtney's arms unashamedly around his neck. She returned his kiss with a fervor that was devastating in its intensity.

Kace, too, was visibly shaken. He abruptly broke the embrace and pushed her slightly away from him. His breath was coming in ragged gasps, and his lips had thinned into a pencil-straight line. He stood up, running a hand around the back of his neck and walked to the middle of the room.

After a moment, he pointedly looked down at his watch, an inscrutable mask slipping over his face. He then turned toward her and spoke. "I'd better take you home." He paused, obviously still shaken. "Tomorrow will be a long day for you."

Courtney swallowed hard trying to fight back the tears that threatened to spill forth. She did not want to go home; she did not want to go to sleep. She wanted to spend the entire night making love to him. But she did not say so. To speak so openly and bluntly of her desire was totally beyond her capacity.

Courtney managed somehow to keep her voice on an even keel. "I'm ready when you are," she declared, forcing herself to look him squarely in the face.

He hesitated for a moment and then with an under-the-breath expletive gestured for her to precede him to the door.

Courtney now felt hysteria laced with anger bubbling just behind her composed facade. But anger triumphed as she climbed into the car beside Kace, a lethal silence deadening both their tongues. How dare he treat her in this manner? she fumed inwardly. There was no doubt about it, Kace wanted her and she knew it. There were times when she felt she could actually reach out and touch the fire that blazed from his eyes. Then why was he so intent on bringing her to the heights of passion only to plunge her into the depths of despair the next moment? She abhorred being used this way. Was it perhaps another way of trying to force her into making a commitment?

With the next thought, she felt as though a giant pair of tweezers were squeezing the life out of her heart. Could it be possible that he was indeed tiring of her as she had already begun to suspect? Immediately, her heart cried *no*, but her mind said *yes, yes, it's possible*.

Anger as well as uncertainty continued to simmer underneath as Kace killed the engine and walked her to the front door. There were just too many questions and not enough answers. But, strangely enough, her mind shied away from delving too deeply for the answers.

With a grim expression on his face, Kace muttered, "I'll pick you up around ten in the morning. All right?"

Following a lengthy pause, Courtney nodded, not trusting herself to speak.

"Good night," he delivered softly before turning and bounding down the steps.

Courtney remained where she was until the taillights of his car faded into the night.

The next morning, Courtney awakened with a pounding headache. After finding no relief from consuming several cups of coffee, she swallowed two aspirins, hoping that by the time Kace arrived she would be feeling better.

If she had good sense, she would cancel the outing, she had told herself over and over. But her heart continued to be the victor over her head.

As she dressed, her mind recalled the painful moment she had compared Kace and being in his company to riding on a roller coaster with no brakes. The predicted collision seemed inevitable now. With shaking fingers, she applied her makeup and then donned a sweater dress. Knitted of a soft silk blend in muted stripes of alternating off-white and tan, it made for a sensational impact. A pair of comfortable sandals and a cream-colored jacket completed her outfit.

Kace was punctual as usual; she met him at the door

ready to go. She was filled with uneasiness concerning his mood, but after seeing his smiling face and twinkling blue eyes she knew that, for today at least, he had reverted to his old self.

"Good choice," he said, frankly approving of her attire. "If my daughter can keep up the pace, there won't be enough time to change clothes before dinner."

She smiled. "I figured that might be the case. So I came prepared for anything and everything."

"You look beautiful," he returned huskily, his eyes taking in every detail of her trim appearance.

Courtney glowed in response to his gleaming admiration.

"You don't look half bad yourself," she threw back at him shyly. And he didn't. He wore a pair of jeans with a lightweight long-sleeved sweater. She noted again the easy distinction with which he wore his clothes.

Bob and Susan were waiting in the car and seemed genuinely glad to see Courtney. There was nonstop chatter among them all the way to the French Quarter. Kace parked the car adjacent to Royal Street.

No matter how often she visited the old section of town, she never tired of it. With Shrove Tuesday and Mardi Gras approaching, excitement was in the air. For the past two weeks, floats and bands had lined the streets along with dancing and torchlight parades.

It had been some time since she had actually participated in the merrymaking of the Mardi Gras season. All the pageantry and hullabaloo associated with the event was geared more for the tourists than for the actual residents.

Courtney's favorite haunts were the curio and antique

shops on Royal Street and the side streets that were lined with art galleries, perfume shops, sidewalk cafes, and tearooms. What she took for granted and passed without a second thought were the narrow, quaint streets and the houses that were standing flush with the sidewalks. These historic buildings were French and Spanish in design with lacy balconies overlooking the street from the upper stories. Their railings of wrought iron led into the houses by way of floor-to-ceiling French windows. Anyone who saw them for the first time would definitely be impressed.

"I would love to take part in the final celebration this coming Tuesday," grinned Susan as they strolled leisurely down Royal Street, "but I'm afraid my tummy might get in the crowd's way."

Courtney laughed outright at Susan's statement. "Much as I hate to admit it, you may be right," she said, her eyes dancing mischievously.

The infectious sound of her laughter drew Kace's eyes to the curve of her lips, to the light shining from her eyes. She looked up at him in time to see something flare up in his eyes, some inexplicable emotion that caused her breath to quicken, and then it was gone, leaving her wondering if it had been her imagination.

"Come on, you two. Quit lagging behind," Susan teased, breaking into the intimate moment. "If I'm to follow the doctor's orders, we're going to have to get the lead out of our feet," she added with mock severity.

A frown marred Courtney's face as she and Kace hurried to catch up. "What did your doctor tell you to do?" she asked.

Susan rolled her eyes heavenward. "Would you believe—walk." She laughed. "He wants me to walk morning, noon, and night."

148

Courtney's eyes filled with sympathy. "When exactly is the baby due?"

Before Susan could reply, Bob cut into the conversation with a grin. "My dear wife thinks she has another month, but the doctor told her it could come any time now."

9

What!" cried Courtney, an incredulous expression mirrored on her face. "You mean there's a chance you could have your baby any time and you're here with all this crowd, shopping?"

"Is what Bob said true, kitten?" Kace followed quietly. He hadn't spoken until now. But his face showed immediate concern. He wanted an answer.

"Oh pooh, Dad," Susan laughed, "don't get yourself all upset. Although I might look like I'm going to deliver any minute now, I can assure you and Courtney that I'm not. I've never felt better. Bob's just trying to start something." Her eyes pleaded with her father. "Trust me, please."

Kace seemed to relax under her calm assurance. "All right, we'll play it your way. But if you begin to feel the least bit tired or uncomfortable, you had better let us know." He turned toward Bob. "Does that meet with your approval?"

"It's fine by me," Bob replied, draping his arm around his wife's shoulders. "She's calling the shots."

Courtney was convinced they must have looked in every antique shop on Royal Street. From there they strolled around Jackson Square and down Pirate's and Cathedral alleys, viewing the artists' works that were on display.

They stopped later in the afternoon for refreshments and spent the time before they were served laughing and talking.

Courtney was conscious of Kace as he sat close to her. His distractingly masculine scent filled her lungs with every breath she drew. Several times her attention wandered from the conversation as she found herself watching in fascination as he wrapped his long supple fingers around his glass.

The rest of the afternoon passed in much the same way. Kace was in fine humor, teasing Courtney every chance he got. His strange behavior of yesterday seemed like a dream. She couldn't have asked for him to be any more attentive. She wasn't at all surprised when his hand slid caressingly down her arm and caught her hand in his.

Susan finally began to tire, although she hated to admit it. It was agreed upon by all to eat an early snack at Al Hirt's Place on Bourbon Street and then call it a day.

After being seated in the boisterous club, Courtney and Susan laughingly tossed their packages at the men and made their way to the ladies' lounge.

"Whew! I'm beat," Courtney exclaimed. She pulled a comb out of her purse and began pulling it through her tangled curls. "Where in the world do you get all your energy? I just don't understand it, especially with the extra load you're carrying."

Failing to get an answer to her question, Courtney turned toward Susan. What she saw made her freeze in her tracks. Susan was bent over double, clutching her stomach and gasping for breath.

Events from that moment on passed in a blur for Courtney. However, there were certain aspects of the evening she would remember always with stark clarity. Somehow she managed to make Susan more comfortable on the floor before leaving her and running for Kace and Bob. What could easily have turned into mass confusion did not. Kace took complete control of the situation, getting an ambulance to the scene in what seemed like only minutes to Courtney.

Bob hovered over Susan while she continued to be doubled up with pain and the paramedics gently lifted her onto the stretcher and into the ambulance. Bob rode with her, leaving Courtney and Kace to follow in the car.

The drive to the hospital seemed endless to Courtney. Tears gathered in her eyes as she stared mutely out the window watching the twinkling lights of the city. Kace was impersonal and remote as he wheeled the car down the freeway as fast as the law would allow.

By the time they pulled into the emergency room parking area, Susan was already being examined behind closed doors. Bob, gaunt and shaking, remained outside the door waiting with bated breath for the verdict from the doctor on call.

When the doctor did come out a short time later, he ushered them into a quiet room adjacent to emergency.

He told them that Susan was in labor with complications and that in all probability he would have to deliver the baby before morning. He added, however, that as far as he could tell, both mother and baby should be just fine, if the complications didn't worsen.

Constant tension and worry followed them like a shadow as they waited far into the wee hours of the morning. Courtney couldn't bear to just sit, so she kept the trail hot between the cafeteria and the waiting room, providing them with cup after cup of hot coffee. Several times she would catch Kace's eyes resting on her face. She could see the agony reflected there, and she felt totally frustrated and helpless at not being able to do something.

At one point he had beckoned her to come and sit beside him on the couch. He had put his arm around her and held her close for a moment. From then on, Courtney remained by his side.

Courtney knew that Susan was in the best of hands and that everything possible was being done for her. Kace had seen to that. Due to his influence, Susan was surrounded by an excellent team of doctors. Still the waiting was painful.

Finally, at four o'clock, a smiling Dr. Wainwright came through the swinging doors and informed Bob and the rest of the exhausted party that he had a bouncing five-pound two-ounce baby girl. And that mother and daughter were both doing fine.

Bob and Kace embraced in silent thankfulness, and then reached out to Courtney, pulling her into their happy circle. Afterward, both father and grandfather beamed and congratulated each other until Bob was allowed to slip into Susan's room.

After Bob left them, Kace turned to her. "Let's go home," he murmured tiredly.

By the time Kace had maneuvered the Mercedes into her driveway, Courtney was finding it difficult to keep her eyes open. He obviously had something on his mind because he put the car in park and rested his head against the seat. The even purr of the engine kept the silence at bay. Still he did not speak.

Courtney could see from the muted glow of the street light the lines of exhaustion that were etched deep into his face. In spite of everything that had happened, they had a lot to be grateful for, she thought. She felt so much closer to Kace. They had shared pain and trauma only to have it overshadowed by the miracle and wonder of birth. A glow of warmth and contentment now surrounded her heart.

Hesitantly, she spoke. "Are—are you going to stay at the hospital most of today? That is, after you get some sleep," she added, her voice sounding tired but happy.

He sighed and opened his eyes. "No, unfortunately I won't be able to." He paused, shifting restlessly in the seat. "If Susan is still doing okay, I have a plane to catch this evening."

Courtney smothered a cry of pain. "Where are you going?" she asked with a waver in her voice.

"To China," he stated briefly.

"Oh, I see," she whispered.

But she didn't. Her heart had plunged to her toes at Kace's unexpected announcement. Sitting motionless as a statue, she felt genuine despair creep over her.

Why had he waited until now, of all times, to make his plans known? she wondered bitterly.

"No, you don't see," he murmured savagely. "That's

154

the whole damn problem, you don't see and never have!"

Courtney stared at him wildly while anger flowed through her veins like ice water. "What exactly do you mean?" she spat back at him.

Suddenly his shoulders sagged as if the fight had gone out of him. "I'm sorry. Just forget what I said," he expressed wearily. "I'll call you before I leave."

"Don't bother," she ground out through clenched teeth, at the same time averting her head. She refused to let him see the tears that had gathered around her eyes.

"I'll call you," he repeated, ignoring her outburst. He then turned off the engine and came around to her side and opened the door. He saw her safely into the house, where tension was thick between them. She looked up at him, not knowing what else to say or do. Then wordlessly, Kace pulled her close in his arms and kissed her with such fierce passion that it astounded her. Without a word of goodbye, he turned and left her standing like a zombie as he walked out the door, closing it firmly behind him.

Somehow she dragged herself to bed, where she cried until exhaustion finally plunged her into a deep sleep.

Ten days. It had been ten days since Kace had boarded the plane for China. The days had passed slowly for Courtney, though she had more than enough work to keep her busy. But she couldn't seem to concentrate on her work or anything else. As the days passed, her spirits sank lower and lower. She missed Kace, but it was more than that. It was their relationship as a whole that preyed on her mind—that kept her thoughts in a turmoil.

She knew he was running out of patience. His behavior the night he left her house so abruptly and the curt phone call the next day had proved it. If only she wasn't so afraid to give herself, to try the commitment of marriage. But she couldn't, not right now. For trust was the name of the game, and as yet she hadn't learned to play it.

She needed proof from Kace that she was more than just another episode of passing fancy in his life. If he did manage to convince her of this, would she in turn be able to do her part? Could she adjust to being part housewife, part career woman? Could she trust him not to seek out other women if she wasn't always there?

These questions rattled around in her brain until, at times, she thought she would scream. But the answers still eluded her. She needed more time. It was that simple. She wasn't ready to play the traditional woman's role. Not yet.

As the ten days stretched into nearly three weeks, Courtney's life became steadily more complicated. There were still problems with one of the machines at the office. It kept shorting out. As a result, she and Amy were behind on several contracts. She wasn't sleeping well, nor was she eating as well as she should. She hadn't heard one word from Kace since he left. It was a foregone conclusion now that he was punishing her, and she bitterly resented it.

It was with both relief and delight when she received a surprise visit from Susan. She welcomed any distraction that would take her mind off Kace.

"I can't believe you're already up and traveling," Courtney exclaimed excitedly, as she stood aside to let Susan enter.

Susan laughed. "I can't either, but Bob had to come to New Orleans on business, and I persuaded him to let me ride with him. Bob's mother has the baby."

"I'm so glad you did," Courtney returned warmly. "Have a seat, while I fix us a cup of coffee. And then I want to hear all about the baby."

"All right," laughed Susan, motherly pride beaming from her eyes.

Although Courtney had visited Susan in the hospital, she hadn't seen or talked to her since she returned home to Lafayette. A dose of Susan's cheerfulness was just what she needed.

Shortly, they both had a cup of the steamy liquid in their hand and the nonstop chatter began. Courtney learned that baby Tamara was indeed perfect. She looked at pictures which proved it.

"Now," Susan said, after placing the photos back in her purse. "I want to know how you're doing."

"I'm fine," Courtney laughed. "I'm the one who should be asking you that question."

"Well, I feel just great. Getting better every day."

Courtney's voice was warm. "I'm so glad. You gave us quite a scare for a while there."

"I know," Susan admitted, "but thank goodness, that's all in the past." She shuddered. "I still don't know to this day what caused me to start hemorrhaging."

Courtney took a deep breath. "That may be something you'll never know."

"You're probably right," Susan acknowledged with a sigh.

A silence followed as they both paused to sip on their coffee. As Courtney surveyed Susan over the rim of her cup, she sensed that her visitor had something else on her mind. A look of uneasiness had settled across her features. She wasn't at all surprised at Susan's next comment.

"I know what I'm about to ask is none of my business," she began hesitantly, "so don't feel bad if you don't want to answer me," she rushed on to say.

Courtney sat her cup down on the table and looked directly at Susan. "Go ahead, ask me anything you want to."

Susan's tongue nervously circled her lips. "Are you planning to marry my father?"

Her question came as no surprise to Courtney. "No," she sighed. "At least not anytime soon."

Susan's face fell. "I thought that might be the case, but I wasn't sure."

Courtney bristled. "Did your father discuss our relationship with you?"

"No. Absolutely not," Susan assured her hurriedly. "But I knew something was wrong with Daddy before he left. You know, of course, he came by the hospital to see me."

Courtney nodded in the affirmative.

"Even though I still felt rotten," Susan continued, "I could sense that something other than me had upset him." She paused to lick her lips. "I've talked to him every day on the phone, and I can still feel all isn't right. He seems worried, concerned." She shrugged. "Maybe those aren't the right words to adequately describe the vibes I've been getting, but I do know he's different," she stressed in conclusion.

Courtney's face grew shadowed. "I have to admit your father isn't too happy with me right now. To be perfectly honest, he's trying to push me into marrying him."

"And you don't want to?" Susan questioned softly.

A heartfelt sigh escaped Courtney. "That's only part of

it. You see, Susan, your father's had the luxury of living quite a few more years than I. He's had a fulfilling marriage, a child, a grandchild, and ten years to gain a reputation as a known womanizer."

"That's not true!" Susan cut in emphatically.

Courtney lifted an eyebrow. "Oh, really?"

Susan's face flushed with color. "Well, I know Dad's dated a lot of women since my mother died," she said defiantly, "but to my knowledge, he's never blatantly flaunted his affairs."

Courtney shrugged. "That may very well be true. But that's beside the point."

"What is the point, then?" Susan asked bluntly.

Courtney thought for a moment before answering. "I've spent most of my adult life working. I've dated no one seriously. And I've become terribly independent." A bleak smile curved her lips. "I'm not at all sure I could conform to marriage. I'm afraid it may already be too late," she added bitterly.

Susan sighed. She felt so helpless. If only there was some way she could help.

"Don't worry about it." Courtney spoke again.

"I'm not," she lied.

Sensing she had said too much, Courtney abruptly switched the conversation to more general topics until Bob arrived.

Shortly afterward, Susan and Bob took their leave, extracting a promise from Courtney to visit them soon.

The day before Kace was due to come home, Courtney decided to go to the office early. As she unlocked the door and stepped inside, she stopped dead in her tracks.

Her hands flew up and covered her eyes as she gasped for her next breath. But when she removed her hands, nothing had changed.

"Oh no! Oh no!" she wailed aloud pitifully as she stood in shocked horror and looked at a room that was filled with computer paper. It was everywhere. The entire office was literally knee deep in it.

For a full minute, Courtney was unable to move. Her legs felt as if they were made of stone. She clenched and unclenched her fingers as tears of frustration filled her eyes and clogged her throat.

Finally she forced herself to take a tentative step further into the room, hearing the papers crunch under her feet as they bore the brunt of her weight. Then she halted again as she eyed the culprit in the corner of the room.

The machine that had given them trouble all week sat proudly, mocking her as it continued to calmly spit out paper after paper.

"Oh, Amy, how could you?" she cried in total despair. "How could you do this to me—to us?" For it was apparent that Amy, in her haste to get away for a much-needed holiday, had forgotten to call and have the service man come and disconnect it.

Courtney was weeping in earnest now as she slowly plowed her way through the rubble in order to get to the errant machine. Upon reaching it, she immediately pushed the off button several times, but, as she expected, nothing happened. She quickly punched other switches hoping against hope that maybe the wires were crossed and that one of the buttons would surely stop it. But no, the machine kept purring, and the lights kept flashing and seemingly laughed at her for making an attempt to halt its actions.

"Damn!" she muttered as the papers continued spewing forth from the silver-tongued monster. There was no way she could unplug it either, because the plug was in the back jammed against the wall. It was much too heavy for her to move.

So in a frenzy of frustration and anger, Courtney kicked the huge device several times. As a result of her action, it retaliated by advancing its speed and cranking the paper out even faster than before.

It was a sure thing now that every contract in the machine was damaged or lost—Kace's most assuredly. And his companies were by far the most important.

Suddenly it was all too much. The mess, plus her worry over Kace, finally broke her spirit. She crumpled to her knees, angry sobs raking her body. She then scooped up a handful of the debris and wadded it up in her hands, her sobs becoming louder.

This was how Kace found her.

"Damn it to hell! What's happened in here?" His voice shook the room like a loud clap of thunder. "Please for God's sake, tell me there aren't any of *my* contracts in all this mess?"

Courtney, realizing she was no longer alone, jumped up and whirled around. Her eyes were wild and haunted as a deer when she confronted Kace standing in the door, his statue unyielding. Although she had recognized the honey-toned voice, he had nevertheless frightened her, he being a day early.

Kace thought, as he took in Courtney's stormy disarray, that she had never looked lovelier. The shimmering brightness of her eyes and the thudding outline of her breast silhouetted against her shirt caused his breath to quicken. He let his eyes feast on her, drinking in the sight of her body, thirstily. He realized more than ever how much he had missed her, wanted her. To hell with the contracts, the mess, and everything else! Nothing mattered now except holding her in his arms.

Still Courtney did not move. Kace, his expression softer, began to walk purposefully through the papers toward her. It was as if she were mesmerized by his presence. But when he reached out a hand to touch her, she snapped out of her stupor, lunging backward before his hand could as much as graze her arm.

"Don't you dare touch me!" she cried, the tears rolling down her cheeks.

For a moment Kace was taken aback at her violent outburst and reaction to him. But his rigid control immediately resurfaced, blanketing his face with calm indifference.

"All right, I won't touch you," he stressed, his voice low and even. "But at least let me see if I can help salvage something out of this mess."

Courtney shook her head negatively but did not speak. She was afraid to speak as well as move. Seeing Kace like this had added insult to injury. Not only was he a day early, but to catch her here in the office surrounded by this ungodly horror was more than she could handle. This was not at all how she had envisioned their reunion.

His attitude also left a lot to be desired. Not one word of greeting had crossed his lips, much less an apology for not calling her the entire time he had been gone. No. All he was concerned about was the fate of his contract. Well, to hell with him and the contracts, she thought bitterly.

It no longer mattered that the sight of his tall lanky frame slouched against the door had made her instantly aware of how much she had missed him and how much she longed to throw herself in his arms.

Nothing mattered now except getting her emotions under control. She knew she was overreacting. Her nerves reminded her of a tennis racket that had been strung too tight, capable of popping at any time.

While she was buried deep in her thoughts, Kace had taken matters into his own hands. He had gone over to the machine and had it pulled away from the wall. He was just bending over to examine it when she found her voice.

"Go away, Kace. Just go away," she said dully. "I don't need you now." The moment the words passed her lips, she wished she could recall them. But it was too late.

Kace, with quickness of lightning, slammed the lid down on the machine, and crossed the room in two gigantic strides. His face was carved of stone—cold and withdrawn.

Courtney stared at him, terror reflected on her face. She thought, for a moment, he was going to strike her. Instead he grabbed her and jerked her tightly against him. She felt the heat of his body envelop her and smelled the clean fragrance that was always a part of him. His kiss when it came was savage in its intensity. Teeth ground against teeth as Courtney struggled to free herself.

It was her bid for freedom combined with her whimpers of pain that finally penetrated Kace's tormented senses. His hold on her slackened immediately as he strove to replace untamed violence with burning gentleness.

When his darting tongue began to gently stroke her teeth and move to tickle the inside vulnerability of her mouth, she was lost. Lost in a vortex of sensual pleasure so forceful that it almost took the top of her head off.

In that moment, she ceased to fight. Her body began to respond to him as a warmness swept through her veins. Suddenly she knew that she wanted Kace as much as he wanted her. Hadn't most of her problems these last few weeks stemmed from being without him? From not feeling his lips, his arms? Then why deny herself this stolen moment of passion? It could very well be her last.

"Courtney?"

There was complete silence in the room now except for Kace's labored breathing.

She looked at him, making no attempt to mask the desire that was burning deep within her.

Kace's mouth suddenly became dry and his hand actually trembled as he slowly urged her toward the floor. They melted together almost as one, using the sea of papers as their bed.

The loud crackle of the papers did nothing to break the spell as their bodies buried deep within them. Kace leaned over her, fusing his lips to hers in a long, passionate kiss.

"Since I've been gone, I've thought of nothing but you," he said hoarsely as he pulled away and looked down at her. "You're like a drug in my blood." Then he bent again and kissed her.

Courtney felt a fire begin to smolder inside of her as Kace's fingers unbuttoned her blouse and then snapped open the catch on her bra. Her breasts exploded free from their confinement, only to become encased once again by his hands and mouth. He worshipped the ivory globes until they were brought to pulsating fullness from his caresses.

The fires of passion that lay smoldering now threatened to rage out of control as his hand left her breast and wandered downward where it slipped under her skirt and began to gently knead her thigh.

She kept her eyes shut tightly as he stripped her clothes from her body. She heard his deep sigh of contentment as she opened her eyes in time to see him devour her body.

Before taking his place beside her, Kace hastily removed his own clothing. In the muted glow of the dimly lit room, she reveled in his nakedness. She felt electric currents shoot through her body as she treated herself to a free perusal of him.

"Kace," she whispered achingly.

"Shhh, don't talk." He opened his mouth on her nipple, teasing it, and she shivered, her fingers in his hair. Aroused deeply by his mouth scorching her skin, Courtney lazily, maddeningly glided her hands down his sides, across his back, around over him, and back up again.

"Oh, yes," he rasped as he reached to slowly part her thighs, where he gently praised the center of her being. The intimacy of touch left her weak, turned her bones to liquid.

"Together, Courtney." His words floated down to her. "Now . . . together."

Before Courtney realized it, he had penetrated her— not fiercely or even impatiently, but with a slow deliberate movement that locked them together in an inescapable passion. Lips and tongues touching, they moved as one in a slow, agonizing rhythm which brought them together in an explosion of passion so intense that it threatened to destroy them both.

It was a while before Courtney or Kace moved. The

force of their lovemaking had taken its toll on both of them, leaving their bodies sated and their minds drained.

When Kace finally disentangled himself, he stood up and reached for his clothes all in one motion, the full impact of the situation hit Courtney square in the face. Had she completely taken leave of her senses? Had she? Yes, she admitted, she had indeed, for an insane moment, lost herself to this gentle devil.

Neither one spoke as they dressed. For Courtney, it was an effort to button her blouse, her fingers were shaking so.

Shortly Kace turned to her. "You know we can't go on like this, don't you?" His voice was deep, but each word was distinct. He waited for her response.

Courtney walked to the window and began fiddling with the blinds. "I know," she whispered as tears clogged her throat, cutting off further speech.

She could feel the tension in the room. It clung to her like a second skin, almost smothering her, it was so penetrating.

"I want us to be married. Today," Kace declared urgently.

"Why?" she asked softly, turning around to face him.

Her question seemed to catch him off guard. Uncertainty flickered in his eyes for a split second before settling on her face unblinkingly.

"You know the answer to that question already," he expressed wearily. "But I'll tell you anyway. I want you and I need you so much that my guts stay ripped to pieces because of it." His face and voice were filled with raw emotion. "Isn't that reason enough?" he added softly.

Courtney controlled her trembling lips by biting down

on them hard. She turned her back to him once more. No, it wasn't reason enough, she screamed silently at him. Wanting and needing were not the same as loving. If he did not love her, then . . .

"Well, what's your answer going to be?" he pressed, cutting into her painful thoughts.

"Kace, I'm—I'm not ready. I—I need more time. I—" She broke off in an effort to grope for the right words.

"No!" he bellowed.

Courtney again flung herself around to stare at him. Rage had distorted his features.

Seeing her shocked expression, Kace made an effort to get his emotions under control. He raked his hand over his hair and expelled a harsh breath.

"Damn it, Courtney, I'm tired of sharing only moments with you," he said, his voice racked with emotion. "Don't you understand I want us to share a lifetime?"

A sharp stabbing pain tore at her heart, but still she could not commit herself. She was afraid.

"I'm not leaving here until you give me an answer!" he told her adamantly.

Courtney was torn. All the pain and the humiliation of the past as well as doubt of Kace and their future flashed across her mind. A shell of frustration, self-doubt, and torment wrapped itself around her, refusing to release her. It was driving her crazy.

"Courtney."

"Don't push me, Kace!" she lashed out at him, breaking her silence. "Just leave me alone!" She paused swallowing the sob that rose in her throat. "I need breathing room. I can't face the thought of marriage now. Maybe not ever!"

There was a silence as deep as the Grand Canyon

following her outburst. Courtney held her breath waiting for his reaction.

His head snapped back as if she had struck him. She could actually see the pain intermingled with anger seep through him.

"Well, that about says it all." His voice was dead, devoid of all expression. "I won't bother you again."

Courtney stood frozen as the door slammed behind him.

10

She had gone over that scene in her office at least a thousand times during the past month. And each time it still had the power to chill her to the very core of her being.

How long, she wondered, would this emptiness remain inside of her? She worked herself at a grueling pace, accepting any and every contract that came her way. She had even hired a full-time secretary, leaving her and Amy free to operate the machines and do the public relations work that the job required.

In the evenings she went home and collapsed, first on the couch and then later in the bed. Sometimes she would wake up the next morning with the realization that she hadn't even bothered to eat dinner the night before.

She kept telling herself she was better off without Kace—that she did not need him. But after a month of not seeing him, she knew she was playing a fool's game.

Thoughts of him plagued her day and night, so she used her work to escape from her torrid memories.

For nothing had changed. Even if she admitted to still wanting and needing Kace, her problem wouldn't be solved. He had made no effort to get in touch with her. She hadn't heard one word from him since he had walked out of her office. From deep within, she knew her words had banished him forever from her life.

She must, she told herself, try to put her life back together again. After all, she still had her good health, a booming career, and her independence. Those things had been enough once. Couldn't they be again?

A few days later, Courtney took off from work early. She had no choice in the matter. The time had come when she must pamper her weary body. She planned to eat a leisurely dinner and then curl up on the couch with a good book.

She had just gotten out of the shower and slipped into a robe, when the telephone rang. She wondered with a frown who would be calling her at home now. The last few weeks with the combination of her terrible work habits and unsociable attitude she had practically alienated all of her friends.

Hesitantly, she lifted the receiver. "Hello."

"Courtney, this is Michael," a deep voice announced cheerfully.

"Oh, hi, Michael," Courtney responded, warmth now lacing her voice. "What can I do for you?"

He laughed. "Would you believe me if I told you I want you to take pity on me and let me buy you the biggest steak dinner in New Orleans?"

Courtney felt her eyebrows pucker. "Are you serious? Where's Barbara?"

He sighed. "She's taken the kids to visit my parents in Texas for a few days, and I'm about to climb the walls around here it's so lonesome," he added, his voice now edged with depression.

"Are you trying to make me feel sorry for you?" returned Courtney blandly.

"Well, you might say that," he said with another laugh.

Courtney chewed her lower lip for half a second. "Michael," she began, "I'd really love to, but I'd better pass—"

He interrupted her. "Ah, Courtney, come on, be a sport,"' he pleaded good-naturedly. "Anyway, I need to discuss a couple of those contracts I turned over to you yesterday."

Courtney sighed deeply, knowing that she really shouldn't turn him down, but she loathed the idea of having to dress again and go out.

"I can read you like a book, Courtney Roberts," he chuckled. "Quit looking for an excuse and just say yes. I promise you the best food money can buy. So how 'bout it?"

"Oh, all right," she laughed admitting defeat. "You win. You always did know one of my weak points was food."

His deep chuckle vibrated through the line. "I'll pick you up in about an hour. Goodbye."

As Courtney dressed, her thoughts centered on Michael and Barbara Evans. They had been good friends of hers for years, going back to her college days. But it was only recently that they had renewed their old friendship.

Michael had opened a new business two years ago in New Orleans. It had snowballed the last year to such an extent that he contracted with Paper-Work-Plus to take care of the overflow. It was a lucrative contract and one Courtney was proud to get. Hence, her decision to hurriedly get ready for dinner when she really would much rather be curled upon the couch with a good book.

She looked sensational in a silk outfit of a rich deep purple. The crepe de chine asymmetrical blouse and soft-pleated pants made her look as slender and elegant as a model.

Shortly, Courtney found herself being seated in one of New Orleans' fanciest new restaurants in the uptown Garden District. Although Michael had made no reservations, they did not have to wait.

The hovering waiter immediately took their order for a before-dinner drink and left them alone. While they waited, Courtney made Michael tell her all about Barbara and the kids. She found herself laughing and beginning to relax as she listened to his amusing anecdotes.

After the waiter served their drinks and took their order, Michael began a full-scale description of his business problems. He had her undivided attention until she happened to glance out of the corner of her eye at the entrance. Michael's words flew from her mind, and her next breath stuck in her throat. A couple came through the door. She recognized the man instantly.

Kace McCord could hold his own anywhere, anytime, but tonight his rugged good looks drew far more than his fair share of attention. The men threw him envious stares and the women melting glances.

He wore a pale blue suit that showed off to perfection his silver-gray hair. A lovely older woman clung gracefully to his arm. To Courtney, they both looked contented and blissfully happy. She forced herself to meet his gaze as he looked around the room. But he merely acknowledged her presence with a cold nod of his head. Courtney felt both anger and suppressed desire surge through her body.

These feelings were followed by another emotion that had been totally alien to her until now. The truth hit her with such a staggering blow that she had to bite her lip to keep from crying aloud. She loved Kace. It was as simple as counting one, two, three. She loved him. And probably had, long before she ever shared his bed.

Quickly, Courtney averted her head lest he see her heart reflected in her eyes. She then pushed the panic button, realizing that the truth had come too late! It was more than obvious Kace was not pining away from a broken heart. He had never looked better. Venturing another look in his direction, she saw him tenderly seat his companion. He must have whispered something to her, because she laughed radiantly and then smiled up into his eyes.

In that precise moment, Courtney's evening turned sour.

Michael, watching the conflicting play of emotions cross her face, asked with concern, "Courtney, what the hell? You look like you've seen a ghost." He paused drawing on his cigarette. "Does that guy mean something to you?"

Courtney sat motionless, her face as frozen as her body. Her knuckles, where she clung to her glass of Chablis, were as white as the tablecloth in front of her.

"Courtney?" Michael repeated. "Do you want me to take you home?" He leaned across the table and covered her hand with his, peering at her closely. There was a perplexing frown marring his handsome features.

Between the touch of his hand and the waiter arriving with the food, Courtney was jolted out of her stupor. The rich aroma of the food almost made her sick. She drew deep ragged breaths in an effort to get her stomach under control.

She quickly rescued her hand from Michael's warm clasp and placed it in her lap. She gave him a watery smile.

"Courtney," he began sympathetically, "let me take you home."

She shook her head. "No, please, eat your dinner. I insist. I'm fine now, really I am," she lied easily. "I just saw someone I wasn't expecting to, that's all."

Michael eyed her skeptically but didn't try to persuade her to confide in him. He respected her privacy, which she appreciated. It took every ounce of fortitude she possessed to sit there the next two hours and pretend that her life hadn't come tumbling down around her.

A short time later, Courtney found herself alone, alone with a lead weight around her heart and a bucket full of unshed tears. Thank goodness she did not have to pretend any longer, she told herself. She sank onto the bed and cradled her head in her hands. She sat deathly still, trying not to think or feel anything, cushioning herself against the misery she was experiencing.

But nothing could keep the thoughts of him touching that *woman*, the way he had touched her, from ripping her insides to pieces. She felt as if her body was being used as a dart board.

Why, oh why, she berated herself, hadn't she understood a long time ago? Maybe if she had admitted to loving him, things might have been different.

Seeing him again brought back all the longings and desire she felt for him. And it was ironic, she thought bitterly, that with the moment she realized she loved him also came the certainty that she had lost him. It was more than obvious he no longer wanted her. Or needed her. Could she blame him? After all, no one knew better than she how hard he tried to convince her that they belonged together. She just hadn't listened.

Now that it was too late, everything became so clear. It hit her with all the force of a bullet through a plate glass window, sharp and shattering. If she couldn't have Kace, with or without his love, nothing else mattered. Her career, her independence, and her lifestyle all counted for naught.

How long she remained in her soul-searching position she didn't know. But when her hands and arms went to sleep, she forced herself to move. She paced around the room until the painful tingling in her limbs had ceased. She then crawled between the sheets and cried herself to sleep.

After that, Courtney could not seem to bounce back. A quiet sadness had surrounded her like a shield. She couldn't shake it no matter what she did. She lost weight, sleep, and even her will to work. She deemed herself a fool many times for losing her self-respect over a man who had already found someone else to take her place.

One afternoon, two weeks after she had seen Kace at the restaurant, her doorbell rang. She opened the door to find Susan standing on her step.

Courtney's face broke into a fleeting smile which

momentarily lessened the hollowness of her face. "Well, hello," she said. "Come in."

"I hope I'm not bothering you," Susan said, by the way of an apology, "but I desperately needed to talk to you and haven't been able to catch you here at home."

"Well, I have been keeping rather long hours at the office," Courtney admitted, hesitantly. She sensed that Susan was upset about something. She could see it in her face. She knew without asking what it was.

"Do you have a moment to talk?" Susan inquired, not bothering to avert her troubled eyes.

"Of course," Courtney answered, "but what do you want to talk about?" She felt a tightening in her chest cavity as she anticipated Susan's next comment.

"Kace," Susan replied bluntly.

"Oh, I see," Courtney murmured in return. With a sigh, she added, "I guess we'd better sit down."

The moment they were seated, the words came pouring out of Susan's mouth. "Oh, Courtney, Dad really has me worried. Something's terribly wrong with him."

The tightening in Courtney's chest became almost unbearable. "What's happened? Has he been hurt?" she asked urgently.

Susan wet her lips nervously. "No—no, it's nothing like that, at least not yet," she answered, drawing a deep breath. "But I'm positive it has to do with you, Courtney," she added in a rush.

Courtney tried to gather her scattered wits about her. "Me?" she exclaimed, shaking her head. "No, I don't think so," she went on, as she pictured in her mind the other woman clinging to his arm. "Whatever is wrong, I hardly think it's because of me."

"Courtney, please!" Susan was really distressed now.

"I know that you two are no longer seeing each other. Dad came to Lafayette about a week and a half ago. He was a stranger. He was aloof, moody, and evasive." She paused to wipe a tear. "All I managed to get out of him was that he loved you desperately and that—"

"What did you say!" Courtney broke in, her voice a shocked whisper. Before Susan could answer, she jumped up and began pacing back and forth across the carpet. Her mind was ticking wildly.

Susan followed her with large puzzled eyes. "Well, I—I said that he loved you."

"Are you positive he said that?" Courtney had stopped her pacing, and the face she cast toward Susan was tissue-paper white.

"Of course I'm positive," Susan stressed impatiently. "Surely you know that. While my father was seeing you, he was happier than I've seen him since my mother died."

Perspiration oozed from Courtney's palms and her mouth was pasty dry. "No—no, I didn't know," she whispered.

Susan looked totally confused now. "Well, what I came to tell you is that he's disappeared. No one's seen or heard from him since the day he left my house."

"Disappeared?" Courtney repeated abstractly. She was aware she must sound completely irrational to Susan, but her thoughts were filled to capacity with the fact that Kace had told Susan he loved her. But there were still so many unanswered questions, she thought. So much she didn't understand.

"Yes, disappeared," repeated Susan with a deep sigh. "Bob nearly knocked the door down at his house—and if he's there, which I doubt, he wouldn't answer the door.

Also, we've checked with Mark and everybody else we can think of that may have seen him." She shrugged worriedly. "Nothing. We've met a dead end at each turn."

"I'm sure he's all right," Courtney stated, but more than a little concerned herself now.

"Oh, Courtney," Susan moaned. "I can't help but be worried. You didn't see him and I did!"

"I'm sorry, Susan, but I have no idea where he is, unless he's out of town checking on a construction site," Courtney replied, chewing on her lower lip.

Susan shifted restlessly. "I thought about that. But he's always let someone know his whereabouts at all times. It's just not like him to be gone this long without letting someone know," she repeated, with a firm shake of her head.

"There's bound to be a reasonable explanation. I'm sure he's all right. Just don't go borrowing trouble," Courtney advised, trying to make the younger woman feel better. But it was difficult when uneasiness and fright were forming a knot in her own stomach.

"Well, I feel sure that sooner or later he'll get in touch with you. And when he does, you'll tell him to call me, won't you?"

"Of course, you know I will. But there's no chance I'll hear from him," Courtney expressed, once again pacing the floor. "I made sure of that," she added bitterly.

Susan stood up and walked to the door. "I have to go," she said dejectedly. "Bob and the baby are waiting for me in the car. You were my last hope, and I wanted to let you know the score."

Courtney, after closing the door, barely made it to the couch before she broke into unrestrained sobs. During the heart-wrenching hours that followed, her entire adult life flashed in detail across her mind. With it came the awareness that she had let what one man had done blind her vision to the goodness and kindness in another. She berated herself for letting "things" like her business become more important to her than loving and being loved.

In that moment, she knew what she had to do. She had no choice. First thing in the morning, she promised herself, she would try and find Kace. She would do anything to feel his arms around her again. She prayed that she wouldn't be too late. That she would be given another chance.

Daylight was barely peeping over the horizon when Courtney pulled her car into the marina parking lot at Lake Pontchartrain. Her heart was palpitating so fast she had to take several deep breaths in order to slow it down. Gripping the door handle, she made herself get out of the car.

She was positive Kace was on *The Majestic*. She didn't know how or why she knew this, but she did. She forced herself to move in the direction of the boat.

Trembling a little, Courtney advanced the few remaining yards and climbed aboard the yacht. Looking around, she noted there was no sign of Kace at all, but she clung to her first thought—that he was here. Stiffening her shoulders, she went forward to the entrance that led to the downstairs cabins and knocked loudly. There was no answer, and half-impatiently she carefully made her way down the stairs and halted hesitantly outside the door of the main cabin.

Summoning her courage, she called: "Kace! Kace, I

know you're in there. Please open the door. I want to talk to you."

Silence.

Courtney pressed her lips together in frustration as she reviewed the situation. What to do? If Kace refused to see her or talk to her, she would have to leave. Tears of self-pity pricked her eyes, making her blink furiously. She tried the doorknob, but of course it was locked.

Her shoulders dropped in defeat, she turned to make her way back up the stairs, when the door swung open abruptly, and a voice behind her said, "What do you want?"

Almost jumping out of her skin, Courtney spun around to stare at Kace as if she'd seen a ghost. In actuality, comparing him to a ghost wasn't too far off base because that was exactly what he looked like. His face was drawn and haggard with several days' growth of beard darkening his jawline. His loose-fitting khakis stressed the gauntness of his thighs and hips. And his usual immaculate silver hair was overly long and unkempt.

A wave of love for him swept over her as she looked at his dear face, unable to say a word. Her tongue felt as if it were encased in concrete.

"I asked you what you wanted," Kace repeated harshly.

"Isn't it obvious what I want," she finally burst out, her voice coming in short, ragged spurts. "I—I came to see you."

"Why?"

"Why?" She gave an exasperated sigh. "Why do you think?"

"It doesn't matter anymore what I think," he muttered, his nostrils tightening. "Anyway, you've already had your say. Just go away and leave me alone."

His words ripped through her brain with all the force of a bullet—brutal and deadly. Oh God, she felt sick. She was too late. Susan had been wrong. There was no way this cold hostile stranger could love her. But she had to try at least one more time to get through to him for her own sanity.

Forcing herself to swallow the sob that threatened to strangle her, she said again, "Kace, I have to talk to you."

"I told you we have nothing to say . . ."

She didn't let him finish. "You may not have anything to say, but I do!" She caught her breath on another sob. "Please," she implored, "please listen to me."

She unconsciously reached out and touched his arm. She felt an electric spark vibrate throughout her body at the contact. Kace felt it too. He backed away with a sharp intake of his breath. He turned and strode to the middle of the cabin, rubbing the back of his neck with a fierce motion.

Courtney tentatively stepped into the room, taking in the disorder surrounding her. The bed was a total wreck, and there were clothes slung everywhere. On the chest, to her right, sat a bottle of liquor with over half of it gone.

Sensing her presence, Kace slowly turned to face her, his eyes pools of torment. He stood unyielding, watching, not saying a word.

Courtney shut her eyes for a moment, struggling to scratch her way out of the pit of despair into which she had fallen.

Her lips parted. "Oh Kace, I made a mistake . . ."

"Courtney, it's over!" he grated ruthlessly.

"I love you," she countered softly.

His only reaction to her words was to clench his jaws together. She could see the muscles working overtime. He remained motionless, although she knew she had captured his attention. He was not about to make it easy for her.

After what seemed like an eternity, he spoke: "When did you come to that conclusion?" he asked, his lips twisted in a smirk.

Courtney was seeing yet another side of Kace. He was close to becoming a snarling stranger—one who, if she weren't so determined, could defeat her.

She quivered. "The—night I—I saw you with that woman." She blinked back the tears. "I—I couldn't stand the thought of you touching her . . ." Her voice played out as the tears finally gained control.

"Go on," he pressed unmercifully.

"The—the way you touched me," she continued, her voice an agonized whisper. "And I—I realized that I loved you." She paused, linking and unlinking her fingers. "But, but I didn't think you—you loved me until . . ."

"What! Didn't think I loved you!" he spat. "Where did you come up with that nonsense?" His eyes were dark angry pools as they glared at her. In that instant, she was positive he hated her. She felt her thin wall of composure crumble around her. She couldn't take any more. She turned as if to walk out the door, pain tearing at her insides. She had gambled and lost.

Kace, with the agility of a panther, moved to stand between her and the door. He stared at her unrelentingly for a timeless moment and then with a groan, reached out and drew her to him, fastening his hungry mouth on hers.

A weakness invaded Courtney's limbs as his soul-searching kiss deepened. She clung to him in desperation as they sought to become one.

Finally wrenching his mouth away, Kace moaned as he cradled her head against his thundering chest.

"How Courtney," he rasped, "could you have possibly thought I didn't love you?"

"You—you never told me," she sobbed, her words sounding garbled against his roughened shirt.

"Never told you!" he admonished. "I told you in a thousand different ways. I told you with my voice, my hands, my lips, my tongue . . ." Courtney shivered in his arms as his passionately spoken words tore her heart to shreds.

"Oh, Kace," she murmured brokenly, raising her face to his. "I've been such a fool."

"We both have," he confessed softly as he molded his lips to hers. The kiss lasted until he scooped her up in his arms and carried her the short distance to the bed.

It didn't matter that the covers were a jumbled-up mess. All that mattered now was healing the wounds that were deep and severe from their long weeks of separation.

They undressed each other with agonizing slowness. By the time they lay together with nothing between them, Courtney felt like a volcano ready to erupt.

Love mixed with heat and passion filled her as Kace held her close against the length of him. He began to run his hands down her back, coming to rest against the roundness of her lower body. She felt him stir as she moved closer to him.

"Oh, God, Courtney," she heard him rasp before his mouth claimed hers. His searching tongue sought hers with accurate precision, meeting and tasting until desire raged through her body.

Her breasts were crushed against his chest as their lips devoured one another. Finally, Kace pulled his mouth from hers and looked deep into her eyes. She caught her breath at the love she saw reflected there.

Her hand went to Kace's lips and caressed them softly, answering his vow of love with one of her own. He reached out and cupped one of her already taut breasts, stroking it into pulsating warmness. He then moved his head lower, taking the waiting tip of first one breast and then the other between his lips.

Courtney moaned from the havoc his teeth and lips were creating. She had been without him so long that she was desperate for him. Again she heard her own moan rise and spill from her lips as Kace moved lower to taste the soft sweetness of her skin.

She encouraged his worship of her body. It was wonderful to be able to surrender to him, to let him explore her while she lay cocooned in his love.

Soon her hands moved of their own volition, encouraging him to return to the parted invitation of her lips. It was her turn to set him on fire. Slowly she kissed his mouth, then roamed to kiss his cheek, his ear. Her lips followed a path down his neck to his chest where she pulled and nuzzled the hair that met her lips.

Kace's breathing had increased to a hard, irregular beat. "Please, Courtney, I need you. Now!" The timbre of his voice was feverish and full of anguish.

She didn't answer. Instead, she shifted her body blanketing his. With a satisfied gasp, Kace locked them together. She felt him to the very depth of her soul as he proceeded to take her on a soaring journey of pleasure so intense that she cried out in joy, slumping against him when the rapture ended.

Afterward, they stayed close. With their physical hunger now appeased, they were free to open their hearts and minds to each other.

Kace shifted, propping himself up on an elbow. He gazed lovingly down into her face. "I was so afraid I'd lost you," he murmured huskily. "I still find it hard to believe you're here beside me now."

"And purring like a contented cat, too," Courtney laughed, as she raised her hand and began to gently rub the stubble that covered his face.

She noted that the deeply etched lines around his mouth were less tense and some of the gauntness had disappeared. But more important, the twinkle had returned to his eyes, and his voice was again filled with honey-toned sweetness.

Suddenly, a frown creased his brow and narrowed his eyes. "Courtney, who was that man you were with in the restaurant?" A shudder shook his body. "You'll never know how close I came to murder when I saw him cover your hand with his."

"That man, as you called him, is a longtime friend and client, happily married with two children," Courtney explained with a smile.

"Even now, just talking about it, makes me . . ."

"I know," she interrupted softly. "I felt the same way when I saw Miss Perfect clinging to your arm and making goo-goo eyes at you. I felt sick."

"Miss Perfect, too, was a camouflage," he admitted, a wide grin broadening his mouth. "All business and no pleasure, until I saw you. Then I switched the roles, hoping it would spark you into action."

"You certainly accomplished what you set out to do!" she exclaimed. "Which reminds me, was that what you had in mind the night of the party *and* the night the baby was born, sparking me into action?"

Kace feigned innocence. "Me? I don't know what you're talking about."

"Oh yes you do!" she grinned wickedly as she reached up and yanked a whisker.

"Ouch!" he yelped. "Okay, you win. I'll confess."

"I'm waiting."

Suddenly, he became serious. "Leaving you those three weeks tore my guts out, but I was hoping if you missed me badly enough, you just might make a commitment."

"Oh, Kace," she whispered achingly, "at first, I thought you no longer wanted me . . ."

His eyes darkened. "Never that, my love, never that," he groaned thickly. "As long as I have breath, I'll want you."

She drew an unsteady breath. "I know that now, but it took Susan's visit to open my eyes."

"Remind me to congratulate my daughter on a job well done," he chuckled.

"Me too," she said happily.

His smile disappearing once more, Kace brushed his thumbs along her jawline. "How would you like to become Mrs. Kace McCord, say in about three hours' time?" he inquired easily.

"I'm game!" Courtney challenged, happiness still bubbling in her voice.

His relief was evident as he gave her a quick kiss.

Suddenly Courtney's face clouded. "What about

Susan and Bob?" she asked. "Shouldn't we call them? They're awfully worried about you."

Kace hunched his shoulders. "I know, my darling, but a few more hours won't make that much difference, surely," he pleaded boyishly.

Courtney felt her heart almost burst from happiness. "Your wish is my command, kind sir," she teased, snuggling closer to his warm body.

"How does China sound to you for a honeymoon?" he asked unevenly, his mouth against her temple.

She pulled back and looked at him. "China's fine with me." A gentle smile curved her lips. "I don't care where we go as long as we're together."

"Are you sure?" He paused, his eyes darkening with pain. "I know how you value your career, your independence . . ." He left the sentence unfinished.

For a moment, Courtney knew real fright. "Oh, Kace," she began unsteadily, "don't you know that from this day forward you're first in my life. Now that I know what love and being loved is all about, do you honestly think I'd let anything take precedence over it?" She drew a shaky breath as she bared her heart to him.

"Oh, Courtney, I love you," he told her, his voice thick with emotion. "And let's begin, right now, filling our shared moments with a lifetime of love."

Silhouette Desire

Coming Next Month

Renaissance Man by Stephanie James

Rare book dealer Alina Corey decided to live like the heroine of her favorite Renaissance book. It worked . . . until Jared Troy, a Renaissance scholar, challenged her to leave her storybook world and face a passion as grand as her dreams!

September Morning by Diana Palmer

Blake Hamilton was determined to control Kathryn but keep his heart free. She tried to rebel in the arms of another man, until a furious Blake promised to teach her a lesson she would never forget—plunging them both into a fiery passion.

On Wings Of Night by Constance Conrad

In one wild night of love Cara Williams had abandoned herself to publisher Quinn Alexander. Now she was faced with the prospect of working for him and wondered if she could deny the fulfillment she found in his arms.

Silhouette Desire

Coming Next Month

Passionate Journey by Thea Lovan

In the silver Moroccan moonlight
Phillipa Bentley was swept away by passion for
Raoul Mendoub, who claimed her sweetness
with his plundering kisses. She tried to rebel
but found this dark, enchanted prince had
bewitched her soul.

Enchanted Desert by Suzanne Michelle

Jana Fleming had inherited Santa Fe's most
famous gallery, but she hadn't expected artist
Fletcher Logan to be part of her legacy as well!
Overwhelmed by his touch, Jana knew Fletcher
was her fate and her future.

Past Forgetting by Pamela Lind

Amanda Adams, prim and proper film
goddess, had finally met her match in
Alex Wojyclas, the principal backer of her
latest film. In his arms her icy reserve melted
and she soon found herself giving in to
passion's implacable demands.

YOU'LL BE SWEPT AWAY
WITH SILHOUETTE DESIRE

$1.75 each

1 ☐ CORPORATE AFFAIR
Stephanie James

2 ☐ LOVE'S SILVER WEB
Nicole Monet

3 ☐ WISE FOLLY
Rita Clay

4 ☐ KISS AND TELL
Suzanne Carey

5 ☐ WHEN LAST WE LOVED
Judith Baker

6 ☐ A FRENCHMAN'S KISS
Kathryn Mallory

7 ☐ NOT EVEN FOR LOVE
Erin St. Claire

8 ☐ MAKE NO PROMISES
Sherry Dee

9 ☐ MOMENT IN TIME
Suzanne Simms

10 ☐ WHENEVER I LOVE YOU
Alana Smith

$1.95 each

11 ☐ VELVET TOUCH
Stephanie James

12 ☐ THE COWBOY AND THE
LADY Diana Palmer

13 ☐ COME BACK, MY LOVE
Pamela Wallace

14 ☐ BLANKET OF STARS
Lorraine Valley

15 ☐ SWEET BONDAGE
Dorothy Vernon

16 ☐ DREAM COME TRUE
Ann Major

17 ☐ OF PASSION BORN
Suzanne Simms

18 ☐ SECOND HARVEST
Erin Ross

19 ☐ LOVER IN PURSUIT
Stephanie James

20 ☐ KING OF DIAMONDS
Penny Allison

21 ☐ LOVE IN THE CHINA SEA
Judith Baker

22 ☐ BITTERSWEET IN BERN
Cheryl Durant

23 ☐ CONSTANT STRANGER
Linda Sunshine

24 ☐ SHARED MOMENTS
Mary Lynn Baxter

SILHOUETTE DESIRE, Department SD/6
1230 Avenue of the Americas
New York, NY 10020

Please send me the books I have checked above. I am enclosing $_____
(please add 50¢ to cover postage and handling. NYS and NYC residents
please add appropriate sales tax). Send check or money order—no cash or
C.O.D.'s please. Allow six weeks for delivery.

NAME _____

ADDRESS _____

CITY _____ STATE/ZIP _____

Enjoy your own special time with Silhouette Romances.

Send for 6 books today— one is yours <u>free</u>!

Silhouette Romances take you into a special world of thrilling drama, tender passion, and romantic love. These are enthralling stories from your favorite romance authors—tales of fascinating men and women, set in exotic locations all over the world.

Convenient free home delivery. We'll send you six exciting Silhouette Romances to look over for 15 days. If you enjoy them as much as we think you will, pay the invoice enclosed with your trial shipment. **One book is yours free to keep.** Silhouette Romances are delivered right to your door with never a charge for postage or handling. There's no minimum number of books to buy, and you may cancel at any time.

Silhouette Romances